FEEDBACK

FEEDBACK

Basil Copper

Chivers Press   •   G.K. Hall & Co.
Bath, England   Waterville, Maine USA

This Large Print edition is published by Chivers Press, England, and by G.K. Hall & Co., USA.

Published in 2001 in the U.K. by arrangement with the author.

Published in 2001 in the U.S. by arrangement with Basil Copper.

U.K. Hardcover   ISBN 0-7540-4655-9   (Chivers Large Print)
U.K. Softcover   ISBN 0-7540-4656-7   (Camden Large Print)
U.S. Softcover   ISBN 0-7838-9592-5   (Nightingale Series Edition)

The text of this Large Print edition is unabridged.
Other aspects of the book may vary from the original edition.

Set in 16 pt. New Times Roman.

Printed in Great Britain on acid-free paper.

British Library Cataloguing in Publication Data available

Library of Congress Cataloging-in-Publication Data

Copper, Basil.
        Feedback / Basil Copper.
            p. cm.
        ISBN 0-7838-9592-5 (lg. print : sc : alk. paper)
        1. Faraday, Mike (Fictitious character)—Fiction.
        2. Private investigators—California—Los Angeles—Fiction.
        3. Los Angeles (Calif.)—Fiction. 4. Large type books. I. Title.
        PR6053.O658 F44 2001
        823'.914—dc21   2001039335

CHAPTER ONE

1

It was around half-past five when it began. It had been a humid, stifling day and I'd gotten tired of polishing my butt in my chair and staring at the cracks in the ceiling. I'd let Stella go early and I sat on for a bit, worrying at a few loose ends at the corner of my mind left over from a case the previous month. That didn't do any good so I got up to pour myself another cup of coffee from the percolator in the alcove where we did the brewing up.

It was then I heard the noise. It was a sort of slurred scraping like that made by a shoe dragging over linoleum. It was followed by a hesitant tapping. It was an unpleasant sound, with connotations I couldn't place for a moment. I grinned when I remembered. It reminded me of Old Pew in Treasure Island. Or at least the stage and screen versions I'd seen. I'd heard the elevator come up a few minutes earlier and I guessed someone had either missed their floor and was walking back down or that the elevator was switched off.

I was left with an image of a cripple with a walking stick making his way stealthily toward my door. Something made me go over from the alcove into the waiting room. The noise kept on coming slowly toward my end of the corridor. I wasn't carrying the Smith-Wesson today and I smelt danger somehow. Don't ask me how. It's just a sixth sense one develops in the gumshoe business. So instead of doing what most people would have done and opened the door I did the opposite.

I bent down until I was below the level of the glass and snubbed the catch over to lock it. For once I hadn't got a light burning in my office so there was nothing to tell anyone I was here. I waited for a long minute. There wasn't a noise from outside but I sensed someone was standing still listening. There was an atmosphere you could have cut with a knife. Then the door-handle started turning silently. That clinched it for me.

Anyone on legitimate business would either have knocked or tried to open the door. They wouldn't have tried the silent entry bit. I knew then I had to make whoever was outside think the office was empty. I sat down on the floor near the door and gave my well-known impression of a vacant space.

Another long minute passed. The noise of the traffic came up faintly from the boulevard below. I sat looking at one of the colour views of Palm Springs we had pinned to the waiting room wall and thought what a ludicrous sight I'd have made had there been anyone there to watch me. I looked back toward the door in time to see a shadow pass across the glass. The door-handle turned again. I sat on, thinking of nothing in particular.

A fly suddenly buzzed in the humid silence. I could feel sweat trickling down my collar. I don't know how long I sat there. Maybe five minutes. Maybe ten. I was pretty cramped by the time I'd finished. And I didn't want to look at my watch in case I made a noise. I couldn't have told anybody why. It was just the feeling. Then, as suddenly as it had come, the sensation left me. I knew there was nobody standing outside the door. The ordinary noises of the late afternoon came flooding back. There was that unmistakable atmosphere you have in a room when there's no-one there and you know the place is empty.

I got up and stretched myself. I stared at the door. Then I crossed over and went back into my office. I didn't make any noise that could be heard from the corridor. I stood by the window. I remembered the coffee then. I threw out the stuff in the bottom of my cup and poured fresh. I added sugar and tasted it. It was good. For my brew, that is. Nobody makes it like Stella. I was puzzled at the lack of noise from the corridor. Apparently a cripple had come to my door. But I hadn't heard anyone go away. I took my time over drinking the coffee.

Presently I put the waiting room light on. I went over near the door and listened. I hadn't heard the elevator go down. That meant nothing, of course. In our building things are pretty erratic. The heating goes full blast in summer. When it's wet and chilly nothing comes through. Same thing with the elevator. Sometimes it works, sometimes it doesn't. It depends on the whim of the janitor. I wrote the whole thing off as one of those Great Unsolved Mysteries.

I kept watching the boulevard below. One or two businessmen in lightweight suits drifted out in the twenty minutes I kept tabs on the entrance. That meant anything or nothing. They could have been visitors or the tenants of other floors. I gave it up in the end. It was around seven when I left my office. I locked the door behind me. I kept a pretty sharp look-out down the corridor. There didn't seem to be anyone around.

2

I went down to the elevator. It was working all right. Leastways it came up when I thumbed the button. I opened the door and stopped. I stood frowning at the empty cage. I looked down the elevator well below. Then I slid the door shut. Acting purely on a hunch I went back down the corridor toward the stairhead. While I was doing that someone must have thumbed the button on the floor below because the elevator went down. I was on the staircase by that time because I didn't see who got in. It had already left my floor by the time I got down a flight.

It stopped again the floor below that, I supposed to let someone on or off. I heard a peculiar swishing noise then. It sounded like a tyre blow-out. It could have come from the boulevard but I figured it was in the elevator well. I looked down through the girders but I had an oblique view from here. I was still a ways up the staircase when the elevator stopped at the ground floor. I looked down the well and caught a glimpse of a man in a dark suit. He went out the elevator cage, walking briskly and disappeared across the lobby.

I was on the ground floor when a car gunned out fast from the sidewalk in front of the building. It sounded like someone was trying to take a pound of rubber off the tyres. I got out the entrance just in time to see a black sedan turn the corner. It was too far for me to see anything and I couldn't have read the licence number. Not that there was any reason to. I stood there for a moment, while its exhaust smoke mingled with the smog that made living in L.A. such a pleasure.

I had another hunch then. I went back into the lobby. I went over to the elevator. The mahogany doors were closed. I looked around. The janitor wasn't in sight and the rest of the building seemed deserted. I saw a thick dark trickle start oozing under the elevator door then. I got over and slid the doors back.

Something sagged forward on to the lobby floor.

Something that looked like a sack of old meat someone had left lying around in a slaughterhouse. He was a young man, smartly dressed, with blond, crew-cut hair. Right now he was holding stiffened hands out as though to ward off the heavy calibre bullet which had torn his chest to ribbons. There was a lot of blood, some of it splashed around on the walls of the cage. I didn't get too close to him.

I could see from the rictus of the smile and the staring eyes that he was already dead. I knew then the reason for the swishing noise I'd heard up the elevator well. The merchant who'd gone away in the car so fast had put the silencer right up against his body. The flash had scorched his clothing where it had rested. I looked at him again for a long second. I'd never seen him before.

I couldn't shut the elevator doors so I went on out. I got a couple of blocks away and had a smoke to steady my nerves. Then I found a public phone and rang the law without giving my name and told them where to go and why. Then I collected the Buick from my rented garage and got the hell out fast.

6

CHAPTER TWO

1

'You get some fantastic ideas, Mike,' Stella snorted.

She sat opposite me on top of her desk, swinging one elegant leg and looking at me with very blue eyes. It was cooler today and the sun was shining and it made a gold halo where it caught her hair.

'What's fantastic about it, honey?' I said.

I had the *Examiner* spread out on the desk beside me. A downpage stick gave the details of the elevator slaying of Charles Blomberg. He was apparently an innocuous businessman who occupied an office on the floor below us.

The police had been pounding about the building with their size twelves all morning. They'd been to see me, naturally. Equally naturally I hadn't told them anything. They were led by a Lieutenant Anderson I hadn't met before. He was a gimlet-eyed individual with frosty hair and a square jaw but he seemed decent enough beneath the bark which had passed for his official manner.

But he'd thawed all right when Stella showed. He'd drunk two cups of coffee and I think he'd have stayed for a third if I hadn't made it obvious the City Force had more important things to do. It wasn't until now, after lunch, when the building had calmed down a little, that we'd had time for a talk.

I repeated my question. Stella was frowning at her knee-cap and examining it like it had a flaw in it. It looked perfect to me.

'This theory of yours, Mike,' she said. 'It hardly makes sense.'

'That's what you always say,' I said.

Stella snorted again.

'Let's take it by stages,' I said.

'The cripple doesn't fit,' Stella said irrelevantly.

'Let's leave him out of it,' I said.

'But why are you so sure whoever killed Blomberg meant to kill you?' Stella said.

'Supposing the cripple was a finger man?' I said. 'Someone who was sent up to try the door and see if I was still in my office. He figured the place was empty and went away.'

'You didn't hear him go,' Stella said.

'Let's leave that aside too,' I said.

'Blomberg's not unlike me. He's in his early thirties—like me. And he had the misfortune to go down in the elevator at the time I was expected to leave the building.'

'No-one could have known that,' said Stella with that maddening logic of hers.

'Supposing the cripple was meant to find out?' I said. 'He could have been on the stairs and heard me leave for the elevator. Then he warned the chill expert I was on the way down.'

'Sure,' said Stella rudely. 'He ran all the way to the ground floor on tiptoe so you wouldn't hear his stick.'

'Let's keep this conversation on a high level, honey,' I said.

'There are such things as bleep radios.'

Stella shrugged her shoulders.

'What then?'

'I changed my mind and started to walk,' I said. 'Blomberg got on the next floor down. Whoever was waiting in the lobby didn't know that. He got blasted instead of me.'

Stella closed her eyes like the sun was hurting them. She looked worried for a brief moment.

'You may have got something, Mike,' she said reluctantly. 'But what was the motive?'

'There you have me,' I said. 'I'm only putting up a few ideas. I can't guarantee to explain everything.'

'Like how the cripple had disappeared by the time you got down,' Stella said. 'You certainly didn't pass him on the staircase.'

'He could have moved away from my door very slowly,' I said. 'He could have stationed himself halfway down the first flight. He could have hidden on the floor below until I'd left before blowing.'

'He was taking a hell of a risk,' said Stella. 'Besides, assuming all this preposterous story to be true, why use someone as conspicuous as a cripple with a dragging foot and a stick? That would only draw attention to himself.'

'If I knew that I wouldn't be asking you for advice,' I said.

'Trouble is you never take it,' Stella said.

She stopped swinging her leg for a moment and stared at me as though I was completely crazy. Come to think of it my ideas did sound pretty wild. But I'd had time to think since last night. And I didn't like what my thoughts conjured up. I'm not normally over-imaginative, but I'd broken out the Smith-Wesson I kept in the small bedroom armoury in my rented house over on Park West. It made a nice comforting feel in the webbing holster against my chest muscles as I moved.

And I was pretty sure Blomberg had been killed by accident instead of me. If it hadn't been for pure chance and me changing my mind I'd have been in the elevator. And the killer waiting in the lobby would have had two choices. In which case there would have been two corpses sprawling in the elevator cage. I sighed. I had nothing but a hunch to go on. According to the police reports Blomberg was as innocuous a guy as could be. Robbery certainly wasn't the motive. And there was nothing in Blomberg's background which would explain his blasting.

In my case there might be a motive. Though I couldn't think of one offhand. But I'd sent a number of guys up in my time. And interfered in the plans of others. But nobody I could figure who would have a long memory. Or take a risk like the guy in the lobby had taken last night. I gave it up in the end. There were more important things to think about. Like I was beginning to get thirsty.

Stella must have seen the look in my eyes. She was wearing a grey mini-skirt outfit today that shot holes in my morale every time I glanced at her, and she had a white bandeau on her hair that made her look like a kid of fourteen. Not quite though. Not with that figure. I amended the age to eighteen.

She slid off the desk with a lithe movement and chuckled at my expression. She went over to the alcove without waiting for me to say anything. While I waited for the coffee I smoked on for a bit and gave my brains a beating. I was still sitting there waiting for the coffee when the phone buzzed.

2

Stella put down the coffee cup on my blotter with one movement and picked up my phone with her disengaged hand.

'Faraday Investigations.'

She sat down on the edge of my desk and cradled the phone while I stirred the coffee. I could hear a man's guttural voice reverberating tinnily in the earpiece of the phone. Stella licked her lips and glanced at me.

'We usually like to know a little about the assignment before we take a case,' she said cautiously. 'Would you care to make an appointment at the office?'

The voice mumbled on and Stella stared out through the window at the stalled traffic on the boulevard, saying nothing, her expression abstracted.

'What's the trouble?' I said, taking the first sip of the coffee. It was one of Stella's best efforts. The girl cupped the mouthpiece with her hand and leaned toward me.

'We've got a strange one here, Mike,' she said. 'I don't like the sound of it. You want me to stall him off?'

I shook my head.

'You're doing all right,' I said. 'What's the deal?'

Stella shook her head.

'Character won't say. He says he must speak to you.'

'You'd better let me handle him,' I said.

'He says he knows something about the Blomberg kill,' Stella said.

'The hell he does,' I said. 'Get on the extension and take notes.'

I waited until Stella was in position and then lifted the phone from the desk.

'You took your time, Faraday,' a man's voice grated.

'It is my time, after all,' I said. 'And it's a

beautiful afternoon here in the city.'

Stella held her hand over the mouthpiece of her phone and grinned happily at me.

'No jokes, please,' the voice said.

'You'd better get to it, then,' I said.

'The Blomberg kill,' the voice said. 'You'd like to know who did it?'

'Not particularly,' I said. 'Why don't you ring the police?'

A sort of half-strangled snarl came over the wire.

'You know why,' the voice said. 'The bullet was meant for you.'

Stella shot a quick glance at me.

'I'd already figured that,' I said.

'Then you'd like to know more,' the voice went on. There was a note of triumph in the character's tones.

'Maybe,' I said. 'What's the deal?'

'We ought to meet,' the voice said.

'You wouldn't care to give your name?' I said.

'Either I'm crazy or you are,' the voice said.

I sighed.

'I thought that would be your reaction,' I said. 'What would you suggest?'

'A meeting tonight?' the harsh voice went on.

'No lonely bridges at midnight,' I said. 'I've had some.'

'I got an address you can come to,' the voice said. Around eleven.'

'That sounds better,' I said. 'What's the house?'

The voice ignored my question

'Ask for Caryl when you arrive. I'll give you a ring at ten o'clock tonight and tell you how to get there.'

'All right,' I said. 'I'll give you my home number.'

'I already got it out the book,' the character said. 'Ring you at ten. And no funny stuff.'

The phone went dead.

I put the receiver down and lit another cigarette. I sat and looked at Stella, who was adding something to her notes. She glanced at her wristlet watch and made an entry of the time.

'Well?' I said.

Stella smiled slowly. It looked dazzling.

'You win, Holmes,' she said. 'You sure you didn't bribe some actor to ring up to prove your cleverness?'

'No actor,' I said.

I put my spent match in the earthenware tray on my desk. I put my feet up on my old broadtop and studied the cracks in the ceiling. The air-conditioning was making funny noises today.

'You get a feeling,' I said after a few more minutes had passed. 'That guy was waiting for me, not Blomberg. The character on the phone just proved it.'

'You're not going to meet him, Mike?' Stella

14

said.

Her eyes were wide and her face had a slight expression of shock.

'Sure I am,' I said. 'But not in the way he meant.'

I tapped the bulge in my suit.

'It's an obvious trap, sure,' I said. 'Otherwise he'd have given me the address straight away. He didn't want me to check. If he rings at ten and it's an hour's drive to wherever I'm going he'll have time to make his preparations.'

'You want me to ring Captain Tucker?' Stella said.

She stopped with her hand halfway to the phone.

'When did I ever ask for help from the law?' I said.

'You were glad of them sometimes,' she said.

'You have a point, honey,' I told her. 'But not this time. This is something I've got to do on my own. And my meeting Caryl, whoever he is, is the most direct way.'

'You think Caryl is the cripple who tried the door?' Stella said.

She shivered slightly as she glanced toward the waiting room.

'Maybe,' I said. 'And maybe not. Or he might be the chopper who blasted Blomberg. They made a mess of it. So now they're trying again.'

Stella got up from her desk and came over toward me. Her face looked more worried than I could remember.

'This is just crazy, Mike,' she said. 'You're walking into a set-up.'

'With my eyes open,' I said. 'Or would you rather them come back here? They could walk back into this office any evening.'

Stella shook her head.

'They won't come back yet. There's too many police around. But there's some sense in what you say.'

'Good of you to admit it,' I said.

Stella smiled. She came over and ran a soft hand over the contours of my face. I was lying back in my swivel-chair so she knew I couldn't make any sudden move.

'I'll be standing by the phone tonight if you want me, Mike,' Stella said. 'All night if necessary.'

'Thanks, honey,' I said. 'I'll ring in as soon as I'm through.'

CHAPTER THREE

It was ten after ten when the phone buzzed. I was sitting in the breakfast nook of my Park West house finishing off my second cup of coffee. The phone was in the living room. I got to it fast. It was the same guttural voice again. He didn't waste any time on preliminaries.

'Faraday, you know Cherry Street?'

I said I didn't but I could find it all right. He told me the section.

'Be at 179 Cherry Street as near eleven as you can make it,' he said 'It might save your life.'

'And then again it mightn't,' I said.

He ignored my remarks.

'Come alone,' he said. 'And be on time.'

'I'll be there,' I said.

I put the phone down and went back into the kitchen. It was now 10.15. I finished off my coffee and locked up. I went out to the car-port and slid behind the wheel of my five-year-old powder-blue Buick. I had a large-scale of the city in the dash-cubby. It took me another five minutes to locate Cherry Street. It would take me all of eleven to get there with the nightclub and theatre traffic.

It did. It was almost ten after the hour when I finally hit the section I wanted. I slid the Buick in behind a maroon Chevy with

17

Canadian licence plates and got out. It was a fairly substantial business area and I had to walk a block to find the address I wanted. I had the first surprise of the evening before I got there. There were no shops or private houses; there were two banks; a mortgage company; and a building given over to various marketing enterprises.

The blocks themselves were made of granite or white stone faced with marble at ground level; the windows were high up, mostly with grilles over them. It was a strange spot for the meeting suggested by my caller. I got to 173 before I began to get the point. The building I wanted was another anonymous business centre, built in a semi-classical style. There were lights on one or two floors; they were dim; like the night lights left on for the benefit of janitors and cleaning women.

There were few people around in this section and as the buildings came straight down to the sidewalk the lighting was correspondingly low. It came only from the street lamps spaced about fifty yards apart. I stopped under the canopy of the Loftus Centre, whatever that was, and had a good look around the street. There were only two automobiles parked outside the next address, which should be the one I wanted. There didn't appear to be anyone sitting in them. I padded up closer to make sure.

I made my living by being cautious and I

intended to go on living the same way. I stopped just before I got to 179. It was a fairly dark spot. I broke out the Smith-Wesson and put it in my right-hand trousers pocket and kept my hand round the butt. I had a good look at the opposite building as I walked. I didn't want to be picked off by a sniper on my way in. It sounded fanciful but it had happened too often around L.A. to let me overlook it.

The only suitable windows opposite were high up and the aureole made by the street lights would have made sighting difficult if not impossible. I decided any danger would come from inside the place I was going. I found it a moment later. There was a big set of granite steps going up two flights to a set of glass double-doors under a bronze canopy. A bronze plate on the wall bore the script figures of 179. On another massive plaque at the foot of the steps was the lettering: RUNSTEDT INSTITUTE FOR THE BLIND. I grinned. I was beginning to get the idea now.

I went up the steps three at a time and looked in through the glass door. There was a light burning in a big hallway with a mosaic pavement. I tried the doors. They were unlocked so I got inside and gum-shoed my way across the hall. I got in the darkest part of the lobby and paused to get my bearings. The place was Edwardian style with a lot of stained glass depicting religious subjects; there were

19

mahogany screens; and a marble staircase spiralled up into the gloom.

There was a green baize notice board on one side of the hall. There was no sound in all the building and certainly no sign of anyone. There was a dim light burning over the top of the notice board. I went over and studied it. It gave details of the Institute's activities and the various class programmes; there were some sheets in Braille stuck up on the board too. There was a brass bellpush in a teak surround next to the notice board. It said: Ring For Janitor.

I went over to the bottom of the spiral staircase. There were corridors leading off here, probably to classrooms and lecture halls. The other floors probably contained more classrooms and dormitories. I wondered why they kept the front doors open so late. Then I figured residential staff would want to come in and out. And few people would want to shake down a blind institution. It was a nice set-up for Caryl or whoever he was. If he wanted to make me an accident victim any potential witnesses would be blind. Or ninety per cent of them. Which was pretty good odds.

I heard a faint snick from the head of the stairs then. I flattened myself in against the bottom of the staircase. I had the Smith-Wesson out now. I started edging up round the curve of the spiral, keeping well into the wall. I held the gun in my left hand and strained my eyes to pierce the gloom. It was pretty dim here and it got dimmer the farther I got from the hallway. There was no light on the first floor but some illumination spilled down from the landing of the second floor.

I stopped near the stair-head and eased the Smith-Wesson safety off. I heard another faint click. It seemed to come from down the corridor at the head of the stairs. I got my eyes level with the floor. A faint shadow brushed across the foot of the stairs and disappeared. I got up on to the first floor and down toward the staircase. I moved fast, moving lightly on the balls of my feet, making sure my shoes didn't squeak on the lino.

I stopped halfway toward the staircase. The faint light from the second-floor landing threw heavy shadows along the corridor. I could see a number of doors along the passage on either side. I presumed they led to classrooms or lecture halls. There was a smell of blackboard chalk and stale dish-cloths up here. There must have been a kitchen somewhere in back. I waited until my eyes became accustomed to the gloom.

When I was certain there was no-one in the corridor on this floor I eased down toward the bottom of the second staircase. The light on the second landing worried me. When I got to the top of the stair I'd be in full view of anyone who might be waiting in the corridor. I saw a shadow brush across the light somewhere up top at that point. I brought the Smith-Wesson up, waited.

I could hear my heart pumping gently. Its beat was slightly up with the increased adrenalin flow. I was in at the foot of the steps now, putting my feet with care as I negotiated the first two or three treads. I had got about a third of the way up when I heard a familiar noise. Something scraped across the linoleum, making a slurred scratching. A second or two later there came the tapping of a stick. I grinned to myself in the gloom but all the same I couldn't stop a slight crawling at the base of my spine.

If someone was trying to throw a scare into me he was doing a pretty good job of it. The scraping noise went on as the cripple dragged his foot along the corridor. The tapping echoed under the vaulting of the corridor ceiling. The noise was going away from me, along the passage leading from the landing. I was two thirds of the way up now. The sounds made by the cripple were getting fainter and I covered the last few treads at a run, my feet making little noise on the heavy carpeting.

I paused at the top of the stairs and eased my head around the angle of the wall, keeping low. One light in a frosted bowl shone softly at the head of the corridor. The passage graded away into semi-darkness. Another thin shadow brushed away along the end. I walked slowly down the passage, keeping close in to the wall.

They were dormitories here, numbered from A to D. I knew, because I passed them all. There were washrooms on one side of the passage. Their doors were open and I could see the light glinting on the taps and basins.

The faint sounds of the stick and the dragging foot went on in the far distance. I didn't like the open doors so before I passed each one I crossed the corridor and closed it. Someone might have been hiding inside, waiting to pick me off. I hadn't lost sight of the idea that there had been two people involved when Blomberg got it. I shut the last door in the end. By this time I was almost at the limit of the corridor. I couldn't hear the noise of the stick any more. I stopped by the corridor wall and the silence crawled back in.

I listened for a good five minutes. I could hear heavy breathing coming from the dormitories. I'd heard the same sounds at night in a hospital ward. The odd broken cry but mainly the mumbles and snores of heavy sleepers. This was pretty well the same. I figured the noises were what they sounded to me. The inhabitants of the Runstedt Institute going about their lawful dreams.

The stick-tapping wasn't repeated. I'd got to the last door by now. It was a heavy oak portal which looked as though it might lead to another staircase. The sticktapper might have gone through it. Or he might not. Either way he'd bolted or locked the door behind him because I couldn't shift it. I frowned. There were two possibilities behind the man Caryl calling me. The rendezvous was a decoy to get me out here. In which case the action, whatever it was, was somewhere else. Or the thing was an ambush and something violent was intended to happen.

I wouldn't find the answer hanging around outside a locked door, so I gumshoed back toward the stairhead again. I tried all the doors on my way down. None of the dormitories was locked. Of course, the man with the stick could have dodged into one of them. Somehow I didn't think so. I had a hunch he'd gone through the far door. Mainly because of the acoustics of the place.

The last dormitory was a good thirty feet from the locked door. And judging by the strength of the scraping and tapping the man I was after was way beyond the area of the dormitories. There was nowhere else for him to go other than through the locked door. I got out on to the stairhead and started down. I was in the light here and I must have been half asleep.

I threw myself sideways and rolled down the stairs. There was a sharp noise like an exploding tyre. I'd heard it only yesterday and I knew what it was. Something tore a long sliver of wood from the banister near my head and went humming away into the darkness. I went on rolling down the stairs. I squeezed the

24

trigger of the Smith-Wesson. It made a great roar which went echoing under the high vaulting of the hallway. I saw the slug strike sparks from the marble pavement down below.

I couldn't see who'd fired but I'd certainly scared the hell out of somebody. I could hear feet pounding the staircase. I got another shot off at a shadowy figure which was almost down to the ground floor. There were cries of alarm now and I could hear doors opening and closing on the upper floors. A yellow segment of light stencilled itself across the staircase. I was up now and pounding down toward the first staircase. I hadn't got a target so I didn't fire again.

A man in a dark suit passed across the hall, running very fast. I was on the curve of the last stair, close in to the wall so there wasn't time for a shot. The gun-artist ducked out through the swing-doors. By the time I got to the street I could hear a car going away in the far distance, to be lost among the rest of the traffic noise. I didn't hang around. I went away fast to phone Stella.

CHAPTER FOUR

1

'What did I tell you?' Stella said.

She sat at her desk opposite and tapped with her gold pencil on very white teeth. The sun spilled in at the window blinds and burnished her hair the colour of copper.

'I hate people who always know what's coming next,' I said.

Stella smiled.

'I went there with my eyes open,' I said. 'And I achieved my object. I didn't get chopped.'

'You didn't exactly learn anything either,' Stella said. 'Except that someone who's pretty good with a silencer is also better at running. Where does it get us?'

'Nowhere,' I admitted. 'But at least we know the blind stick-tapper is in league with the pistol artist. Most likely he's an inmate at the Runstedt Institute.'

'You won't be very popular if you go poking around there,' Stella said. 'They probably called the police last night. You must have woken the whole place up. Coffee?'

I nodded. I smoked on, frowning at the smog outside the windows as Stella went over to the alcove to switch on the percolator. Stella came back while she was waiting for the brew to heat up.

'It's funny really, Mike,' she said.

'I'm glad you think so,' I told her.

She shook her head.

'I was just thinking of the set-up. You've never seen the blind man so you wouldn't be able to identify him if you saw him. And he certainly wouldn't recognize you.'

I nodded.

'The blind leading the blind.'

'You coin a good phrase,' Stella said.

I ignored that and after a minute she went back to the alcove.

'You've given me an idea, honey,' I said. 'I have got something to go on. Assume for the moment that the finger-man lives at the Institute. Unless my ears are deceiving me he's got a lame foot. There can't be that many lame and blind men there.'

Stella's eyes were shining. Not with admiration for my reasoning. That wouldn't be like Stella. She was probably thinking over her last crack.

'You feel it would be worth a look back at the Runstedt Institute?'

'It might be,' I said. 'Unless the pistol merchant is on the staff too the lame character wouldn't be able to tie me up with Mike Faraday. I'd be under another name, of course.'

'Of course,' Stella said. 'You haven't got

27

much to go on.'

I puzzled away at the problem while she went over and did the pouring.

'Anyway, the Institute isn't going to run away,' I said.

'Plenty of time to go over there.'

Stella put the steaming cup down on my blotter and went to get her own. I sat inhaling the aroma of the bean. This was really the best moment of the day. Stella was back at her own desk now, stirring her cup.

'We still don't know why anyone should want to kill you,' she said.

'You can't have everything,' I said.

We were sitting there drinking coffee and trying to break the conversational deadlock when the waiting room door buzzer sounded. Stella smoothed down her skirt and disappeared through the far door. I finished off my second cup of coffee and took my feet off the desk. Looked like we might have a client. I could hear the faint murmur of voices from the waiting room. Stella came back with a glint in her eye and cleared the cups away.

'We got a client, Mike,' she said.

'That's great,' I said. 'I need a new pair of shoes. Tailing is murder on the feet nowadays.'

Stella grinned.

'I don't think it'll be like that,' she said. 'The lady didn't strike me as the type.'

I straightened my tie and sat up in the chair.

'What's she like?' I said.

Stella made a little clicking noise. She studied my reaction carefully.

'Too nice for you,' she said.

I grinned back at her.

'What are we waiting for?' I said. 'Wheel her in.'

2

The girl who sat down in the chair opposite my desk was quite something. She was tall and she had one of the most perfect figures I'd ever seen. Her hair was a dazzling blonde. She wore it long and it cascaded down either side of her face in soft waves. She wore a severe black sweater with a white V-stripe that hugged her breasts and made it look like they were straining to be free. She had one of the smallest waists I'd ever seen on a girl and the sweater was held in across her taut, flat stomach by a brown leather belt which sported a massive gold buckle.

She had on white trews of some smooth material that set off her long legs, and brown Cuban-heeled boots. Her forehead was high and broad and her soft brown eyes looked pleadingly at me. For the rest she had a smooth, even tan that hadn't come out of a bottle. Her rich, full lips moved back slowly from perfect teeth in a hesitant smile. She had a rabbit's foot set in a gold mount on a thin gold chain round her neck and she had a plain

29

gold band and another ring with a single diamond setting on her left hand.

She was about twenty-six, sure of herself and the look in her eyes showed that she knew it. She held her right hand in close to her side. Two minute eyes set in crinkled folds of skin regarded me superciliously. The tiny dog licked its chops and turned lazily in its owner's hand. I never did find out what breed it was but, like its owner, it had it made.

'It's all right, Dodo,' the girl said in a chintzy voice. 'The big, naughty man won't hurt you.'

Stella coughed suddenly, like she'd got something in her throat.

'This is Miss Barr, Mr Faraday,' she said hastily.

'I didn't mean to be offensive, Mr Faraday,' the girl said, flushing.

'It's all right, Miss Barr,' I told her. 'I am a big, naughty man. That is, when the occasion's right and the time's suitable.'

Stella grinned and went back to her desk. Her blue eyes searched my face mockingly over the girl's shoulder.

'Would you like a cup of coffee, Miss Barr?' I said.

The girl shook her head.

'No thanks, Mr Faraday. But I would like to smoke if you don't mind.'

'Sure,' I said.

I pushed the earthenware tray over toward her as she searched in a small brown leather shoulder bag. The little dog licked its lips. Its eyes seldom left my face. It looked like it didn't trust me. I didn't blame it. The girl came out with a gold lighter shaped like a vase. She held its shaded flame to the tip of a Turkish cigarette and inhaled the smoke gratefully. I looked at her again. Somehow the face was familiar, yet I couldn't quite place her.

'I've got a bit of a problem, Mr Faraday,' she said, without any preamble. 'I'd like some advice.'

'That's what we're here for, Miss Barr, I said.

I leaned back in my swivel chair while the girl disappeared in a cloud of blue perfumed smoke again. When she re-emerged she seemed satisfied by what she saw in front of her.

'You seem to have a pretty business-like set-up, Mr Faraday. I need someone discreet. Above all he must be strong, tough and reliable. He must be able to take a punch and get up for more; slug it out with the best and come out on top. He must know the law and how to operate in and out of it. I want someone as tough as steel, absolutely without fear and with a brain like a computer.'

'You want Einstein, John Wayne and Cassius Clay,' I said. 'You've come to the wrong shop.'

The girl joined in Stella's laughter.

'I was just having you on, Mr Faraday,' she

said. 'But I wasn't really exaggerating.'

'I just sent my muscles for re-treading,' I said.

The girl's eyes looked at me for five long seconds across the desk.

'Someone's been trying to kill me,' she said.

'That makes two of us,' I told her.

The girl shifted uneasily in her chair and I saw Stella frown over at me.

'It's another matter, Miss Barr,' she said. 'Mr Faraday's got a great sense of humour.'

'I wasn't joking, don't think that,' I told the girl. 'Just exactly what do you mean?'

Miss Barr blew some of her perfumed Turkish tobacco-smoke out through her elegant nostrils. The small dog on her arm blinked in a watery manner.

'I can't go into it all now,' the girl said.

She took a small gold watch out of her handbag and consulted it hesitantly.

'I've got another appointment soon,' she went on. 'I'd like you to come out to my house later this afternoon. If it's convenient.'

'It's convenient,' I said. 'But what's so secret?'

The girl glanced over her shoulder at Stella.

'I have to be absolutely certain that what I say won't go outside the two of you,' she said.

'You have my word,' I said.

The girl nodded. She had a faint smile round the corners of her mouth.

'I already had a thorough check done on

you, Mr Faraday. That's why I'm here. This is where I want you to come.'

She scribbled something on a small gold-coloured scratch pad she took from her bag. She passed it across the desk to me. It was a bridge scoring card. Her address was a place called Gramercy Court in Beverly Hills.

'I'll have to ring you after lunch, Mr Faraday,' she said. 'There are reasons. I'll give you the time to call then.'

'Fine,' I said. 'I'll be around all afternoon.'

'It should be a little after three,' the girl said. She got up from the chair. I got up too to see her to the door.

'What makes you so certain someone's trying to kill you?' I said.

The little dog sneezed. It was either something to do with the sunlight or the smoke. The girl fussed with him for a bit before she turned back.

'I can't be certain, Mr Faraday,' she said. 'But I'm pretty sure my husband's in back of it.'

CHAPTER FIVE

1

'Nice-looking girl,' I said.

I went back to my desk and frowned at the faint traces of Turkish cigarette smoke, which were still rising to the ceiling. Stella had gone over to the alcove and was rattling about with the cups.

'If there's any more of that stuff left I'll have another,' I said.

Stella rattled the cups more fiercely.

'I've seen her somewhere before,' I said.

Stella came out from behind the screen and looked at me pityingly.

'What rock did you crawl from under?' she said. 'That was Candy Barr, the movie star.'

'You'd better change your name to Ella Wheeler Wilcox if you're going to come up with any more lines like that,' I said.

Stella smiled.

'You know the girl, Mike. Billed as "The sweetest thing on two legs".'

'You could have fooled me,' I said. 'I haven't been to the movies much since Ronald Colman's time.'

Stella shook her head.

'You've been missing out,' she said.

'So it seems,' I told her. 'This is where I get

a chance to catch up.'

I put my feet on my broadtop and squinted over at the smog outside the windows. The stalled cars on the boulevard were making a nice exhaust-fume shimmer in the sunshine now. I could still smell the fumes of Candy Barr's Turkish cigarette and beneath it the more elusive perfume of young, tanned flesh and something like cedar. Talcum powder, perhaps? I gave it up. Stella was back now. She put the cup down on my blotter.

'Fresh brew,' she said. 'The other stuff was no good.'

I stirred gratefully.

'You think she was on the level about her husband, Mike?' Stella said.

'I hardly imagine she'd come on over here if she weren't,' I said. 'You'd better look him up in the *Hollywood Directory.*'

Stella ruffled the pages for the next five minutes. I went on sipping my coffee and thinking of tanned young dolls who were being paid millions of dollars for exposing their skins on the screen.

'She's been married two years,' Stella said presently. 'He's an oil executive, apparently. Doesn't give his name.'

'He would be,' I said.

'Insurance?' Stella said.

'Could be,' I said. 'I shall know anyway, by this afternoon. But what would an oil man want with money?'

'They always want more,' Stella said.

'When was her last movie?' I said.

Stella went back to her page-turning.

'Came out a few months ago,' she said. *'Freak Me Wild.'*

I gave Stella a long look. She flushed beneath her tan.

'It's the name of the movie, you goof,' she said patiently.

'Don't tell me we got a new *Directory*?' I said.

'Came in last week,' Stella said. 'Up to date to within the last six months.'

'Pretty good,' I said.

'We haven't paid for it yet,' Stella said.

'Not so good,' I said.

Stella smiled and went on fondling her coffee cup. She got up to get me another. I had a look at my watch. It was just twenty past twelve. I thought I'd go take an early lunch and wait for the girl's call. There didn't seem much else to do. Stella was back now with the coffee.

'Strange, wasn't it?' she said.

'Something threatening her life too?' I said. 'Sure. If you think about it enough.'

I shrugged and went on stirring my coffee.

'Probably nothing in it. These movie dames are always getting screwy fancies. If it isn't the husband it's someone else. Besides, the husband would be pretty crazy trying something on. With the sort of money she's

36

making he's got a permanent meal ticket.'

I decided not to beat my brains out. I'd hear about it soon enough.

I had a quick sandwich and a beer at Jinty's and was back on the job around one forty-five. I sat in the office and went through the last two days' *Examiner*s. There was nothing fresh on the Blomberg kill. But there was a couple of sticks on an inside page about an intruder at the Runstedt Institute who'd been chased by the caretaker. Apparently a couple of shots had been fired. There had in fact been three. They must have been deaf too. I grinned. The story made it sound like I was the pistol merchant.

I guessed the janitor had been covering himself in glory. I didn't want to take away his kudos. I turned back to the *Hollywood Directory* and studied up on Candy Barr. It looked like I'd missed something by not keeping up to date with modern films. They even had a picture of Miss Barr in what they referred to as 'her most notable success'. She looked even better with her clothes off. I sat on smoking until someone rang through from the Barr mansion in Beverly Hills. It would be all right for Mr Faraday to come out at a quarter of four.

I left a note for Stella and went home to change into a clean shirt. I still carried the Smith-Wesson and I kept a sharp look-out on the stairs but there was no-one around.

Neither could I see anyone tailing me on the way to Park West. I ran a shower and fooled around the house for a while. It was just turned three when I left. There was still no-one around that I could spot but just to make sure I took a couple of side turnings and doubled back on myself. It was all for nothing but someone had it in for me and it was time well spent.

2

Gramercy Court looked like about thirty acres of expensive real estate set back behind a massive flowering hedge ten feet or more high. There was a brick-pillared entrance with ornamental iron gates which were closed so I guessed there'd be steel chain-link fencing inside the hedge. They wouldn't have had such massive gates if anyone could have walked through a gap in the hedge. There was a Spanish-style lodge with a green-tiled roof set next the gates.

I sat in the Buick and tooted the horn. The gates opened smoothly, operated electrically from the lodge. I drove into the entrance between the pillars and stopped. A big man in a blue turtle-neck sweater and with a hard face was standing in the door of the lodge with a red telephone clamped to his ear. He had pug written all over him. He looked at me with hard, hot eyes to match his face and said something in staccato tones.

Another big man in drill trousers and a khaki bush-shirt lounged casually at the corner of the building. He had a savage-looking Alsatian on leash and was having a job restraining it. I decided not to get out the car. The second man, who equally obviously, was private army, carried a heavy Colt revolver in a highly polished leather holster buckled to his belt. He nodded at me distantly from under his Texas-style cowboy hat. I waited politely until the first man had finished his telephone conversation.

The man in the turtle-neck sweater looked over at me casually.

'He's here now,' he grunted.

He said something unintelligible and put the phone down. He scribbled something on a pad and wandered over to the Buick. He regarded me silently for a moment. Then he spat a string of tobacco juice down on to the tarmac surface of the drive. The stream made a glittering amber jet in the bright sunshine. I didn't say anything but waited for him. Close up his face made Lee Marvin's look almost tender.

'It's come to something when private dicks got business with dollies like Miss Barr,' he grunted to the second man.

The man in the white-hunter outfit grinned. The Alsatian twisted round on its leash and tried to bite his hand. He cuffed it amiably behind the ears. The dog snarled menacingly. The big man grinned again. The dog was straining toward me, not its handler.

'What's your business, dick?' the man in the sweater said.

'Private,' I told him.

The pug in khaki had a smile like a watermelon now.

'You think you're pretty tough, don't you,' the man in the sweater said.

His voice had gone soft but he was white around the mouth. The big man went on laughing in the background.

'We can easily find out,' I said. 'If you've got five minutes.'

The hard-faced man looked at me levelly for a moment. His eyes were a muddy green, like dirty stream water. They didn't waver as he traded glances with me.

He jerked his thumb at a notice set over the door of the lodge.

It said in red on white: VISITORS MUST KEEP TO THEIR CARS AT ALL TIMES. DANGEROUS DOGS.

'You always stick to the rules?' I said.

The man in the sweater spat again.

'When it suits me,' he said. 'I'll remember you.'

'No effort,' I said. 'I'm always around.'

I drove off while he was thinking up his reply and left him in a cloud of blue exhaust fumes. He had to lift his hand quickly from the

Buick's door to avoid being chopped by the windshield. I grinned at his expression in the mirror. I followed the curving drive around. It was a nice set-up. The road snaked between tropical vegetation and shaded lawns for about half a mile. I saw several more guards exercising dogs on the way up. I noticed the drive was designed to curve in continuous esses. That way the guards could cut off any cars simply by going across the grass. And because of the continuous curves vehicles were restricted to slow speeds. All facts worth remembering.

I came to another mesh-gate across the drive then. I slowed to a halt. There was a small glass cabin outside the gate, a cross between a sentry-box and a telephone kiosk. The door was open and another guard in khaki was lazily taking the sunshine. He leaned on a shelf inside the door and listened to a voice at the other end of the red telephone he held to his ear. He grinned as he saw me at the wheel. He put down the phone and strolled over.

'Nice to meet you, Mr Faraday,' he said. 'Miss Barr's expecting you.'

'Nice to get some courtesy around here,' I said.

The young man in khaki grinned. Now that I could get a good look at him I could see he had a frank, open face. He was about twenty-eight and his blond hair was cut en brosse. He had the style of a Marine Corps sergeant. Like

41

all the people around the Barr estate he looked like he could handle himself.

'You don't want to worry about Fenton, Mr Faraday,' he said. 'He's just there to frighten the tourists.'

'So long as we know,' I said.

The guard grinned again. He went over to the gate and opened it. I gunned up to the entrance and sat with the engine idling.

'The restrictions don't apply beyond this point,' he said.

'No dogs and no guards?' I said.

The blond boy nodded.

'Correct,' he said. 'This is where the social bit begins. Just gardens and luxury living.'

'Sounds all right,' I said.

The boy put his hand up like he was going to give me a military salute.

'You'll find Miss Barr on the terrace,' he said. 'You can't miss it. She already knows you're here.'

'I'll bet she does,' I said.

I drove on through. I could see the blond character staring after me in the rear mirror. Then he closed the gate and started padlocking it. I fought the Buick up the last of the bends, then the terrain was smoothing out and I was coasting the remaining few hundred yards up to the main house.

It made Xanadu look like something out of Poverty Row. The house was modelled on the lines of an 18th-century French chateau. I figured it for a movie star's residence of the immediate post-World War period. World War One, that is. No-one could afford to build a place like it nowadays. There was so much of it that you could only take in a wing at a time. It marched on round behind the trees and disappeared. I stopped the Buick at the foot of a flight of marble steps that wouldn't have been out of place at Versailles.

By the time I got to the top of the flight I was winded. The house had round towers with lead-capped roofs like something out of a fairy talc. There were even cupolas made of copper that time and weather had given a green patina. Like all such fantasies, the architect had got his periods and styles mixed up. It was a mixture of the Kremlin, Topkapi and M.G.M. But it was all right if you liked that sort of thing. I did. There isn't too much fantasy in the world these days. I looked for Fairbanks Senior to come bounding down the steps toward me.

There was a great view of the acres of garden up here. I was on a terrace of flagged tiles that must have been all of a thousand feet long. There were stone benches set about, some fountains with lead figures and a fish pond the size of an Olympic swimming pool. A scarlet figure in the distance waved energetically. Candy Barr looked like a character out of one of her own movies as I got up closer.

CHAPTER SIX

1

The girl looked more like some impossibly groomed beauty ad even than the stills in the *Directory*. Now that I'd boned up on her career I remembered some wag around the studios had dubbed hers as 'The Face That Launched a Thousand Writs'. I knew why. Men fought over her like seagulls tear over a morsel discovered along the shore-line. I didn't know how her husband made out. I didn't want to know. It was none of my business. And I didn't intend to get involved myself.

Candy Barr looked like she knew what thoughts were passing through my mind. She was probably a very shrewd cookie. She'd have to be to survive in the Hollywood jungle at such a tender age. A faint smile turned up the corners of her mouth as she came down the terrace toward me. She held out both arms like I was her long-lost lover in some Ruritanian romance and I had the crazy idea she was going to jump into my arms.

She didn't though. She merely took my right hand in her own cool hands and welcomed me graciously to Pickfair. I had to keep shaking off the movie image all the time I was out at Gramercy Court. The girl wore a scarlet

44

trouser suit that hugged every line of her figure. She looked as elegant as though she was just going in front of the camera.

I noticed she still wore the rabbit's foot charm around her neck. I learned later that she never took it off. There was no-one else around but a girl with a coffee-coloured skin who hovered around up at one end of the fish-pool. In the old days she'd have been dressed in a maid's outfit. Today she wore pale blue slacks and a blue linen sport-shirt. She stood by a portable bar, smiled shyly at me and did something with cracked ice in a cocktail shaker. I thought Candy Barr was going to ask her to peel a grape but she didn't.

'I thought we'd have something cool out on the terrace, Mr Faraday,' the girl said, motioning me over to a cane lounging-chair that looked out of place among all the grand statuary. The Barr girl sank down on another chair opposite and searched my face intently over the glass-topped table between us. The chair was a bit too low for my taste. I looked around for the leopards but maybe it was too early for them to show yet. I couldn't read the expression in the girl's eyes because she wore dark cheaters over them.

'I'll have the usual, Rita,' the girl said coolly, raising herself on one elbow and looking with satisfaction over the acres of real estate below us.

'Can I tempt you with a rum punch, Mr

Faraday?'

'You could tempt me with a coca-cola, Miss Barr,' I said.

The girl laughed and I could see that the coffee-skinned girl was smiling too.

'A rum punch for the gentleman, Rita,' Candy Barr said, taking the long, iced glass the maid held out to her. There was orange peel and slices of lemon and lots of other junk floating around in its clouded depths. The girl put down her glass on the table top and waited patiently until my own drink was mixed. Her small, pink well-manicured hands lay quietly in her lap. She turned from me and looked out across the sloping lawns of the estate again and her thoughts seemed miles away.

The maid put my own drink into my hand and stood back near the trolley.

'I'll ring if I need anything further, Rita,' the girl said.

The girl in blue slacks smiled faintly at me and then walked back across the terrace toward the house. Candy Barr waited until she was out of earshot. Then she raised her glass.

'Cheers,' she said, in the English fashion.

I squirmed up in my cane chair and lifted the glass to my lips. The drink had been mixed just right. It was cold and it tasted as a rum punch should taste. It seemed to make the view twice as attractive. Sitting here with a dish like Candy Barr I could have forgotten all about her troubles. Or my own, come to that.

'I meant what I said in your office, Mr Faraday,' the girl said. 'I'm in trouble.'

She had a disconcerting way of picking up a previous conversation like it had never been interrupted. And she didn't lead up to the subject with a preamble, like most people. Maybe she was still honest over the things that mattered. Strangely, she hadn't been corrupted by many of the hangups that Hollywood always gives people. Though I couldn't speak for her morals, of course. That was her affair. I put my drink down on the table at my elbow and got out my package of cigarettes.

'You don't mind?' I said.

The girl shook her head. I lit up and put the spent match in the box. I feathered blue smoke at the distant ranges of hills and sat back in the chair.

'You mentioned something about your husband at the office,' I said. 'Were you really serious?'

The girl looked at me gravely.

'Never more so, Mr Faraday,' she said.

'We'd better go into this pretty carefully,' I said. 'I'd like to see where I'm stepping. You've been married a couple of years?'

The girl smiled.

'You've been reading the *Hollywood Directory.*'

I admitted it. The girl didn't say anything for a minute, just sat with her hands folded in her lap. She seemed to be intently studying the jets of water in the fountains below. I used the interval to get some more of the rum punch down me and get out my scratch-pad. I jotted some notes while we talked.

'What sort of man is your husband?' I said.

'Roy?' she said.

She wrinkled up her forehead like the question had been a puzzling one.

'Roy Lawrence,' she went on.

'Pretty nice, I guess.'

She shrugged.

'I wouldn't have married him otherwise.'

'I understand he's in oil,' I said.

'He's thirty-three,' the girl went on, as though I hadn't spoken. 'An executive with Tri-State. He's comfortably off, if that's what you mean. He has no real need of my money.'

Candy Barr must have sensed some irony in my glance because she flushed and shifted uneasily in the cane chair. The faint sound of a motor-mower came up from the garden below now. The barbering of these lawns must have been a full-time job, come to think of it. They were a deep velvet green which meant there must have been sprinklers in the turf every few yards or so. And that cost money in this climate.

'You doubt me, Mr Faraday?' the girl said.

'People always need money, Miss Barr,' I said. 'I'm just trying to establish a few facts. You said your husband was trying to kill you.

48

What makes you think that?'

'I'm getting to it,' the girl said. Her voice had a faint trembling.

'You love him?' I said.

'That's a pretty unnecessary question,' the girl said.

I shook my head. I balanced my cigarette on the edge of the glass table where it wouldn't fall off on to the turf.

'None of my questions are unnecessary. I ask if you loved him. I'm still asking.'

The girl pouted. It looked good on her.

'I wouldn't have married him otherwise,' she said again.

'It doesn't always follow in Hollywood,' I said. 'I'll put that down as yes.'

I leaned forward and picked up my glass. Now that I'd got the knack of the chair it was getting kind of comfortable at that. I told myself mentally to knock it off. I was getting used to the life. And I might find it hard to readjust back at the office.

'What about your husband?' I said.

2

The girl fiddled with her tall glass. The sunshine made a dazzling bluish light where it caught the frosted edges of the crystal.

'I guess so,' she said. 'I don't really know.'

I didn't say anything. I made another note on my sheet of paper. The girl turned up the

49

corners of her mouth.

'Does that surprise you?'

'Not really,' I said. 'How many couples really know themselves, let alone each other.'

The girl shot me a mocking glance.

'You're quite a philosopher, Mr Faraday.'

'All part of the service,' I said. 'I don't put it on the bill.'

'Which reminds me,' the girl said.

She put her hand under the table and fiddled about on the rack there. She came up with the small handbag she'd had at the office.

'I haven't asked your rates and I haven't given you a retainer.'

'It's not important,' I said.

The girl looked shocked.

'We all have to eat, Mr Faraday,' she said. 'And I expect to pay for your services. What do you charge?'

I told her the daily rate. She looked even more shocked.

'It's not nearly enough,' she said.

'There I can't argue with you,' I told her. 'Especially for a combination of John Wayne, Einstein and Cassius Clay.'

Candy Barr grinned.

'Forget I said that,' she said. 'It sounds pretty pretentious come to think of it. Especially when my suspicions may mean nothing.'

'We'll see,' I said.

The girl opened up the bag and rummaged

around. She came up with a crisp fan of greenbacks. They made a nice crinkling noise as she shoved them across the table to me.

'There's a thousand dollars,' she said. 'To be going on with. If you need any more for expenses let me know.'

I fingered the fan tentatively. The notes felt nice and solid beneath my hands.

'I'll let you know,' I said. 'I'll get Stella to let you have a receipt for this. Now we talk about your husband.'

'He's out of town for the moment,' Candy Barr said. 'For two or three days. He got the three o'clock plane. That's why I asked you to come out here now.'

'So we've got plenty of time,' I said. 'I know these things are difficult. Talk away like I'm a piece of the furniture.'

Candy Barr's eyes searched my face.

'That's a bit difficult, Mr Faraday,' she said. 'But I appreciate your approach.'

The girl shut her bag and put it back on the ledge under the table. She settled herself back in the cane lounging-chair and picked up her glass again.

'It started about three weeks ago,' she said softly, like she was speaking to herself instead of to me. I put the sheaf of bills in my wallet and put it back in my pocket. It made a nice glow there against my suiting. I sat waiting for her to go on. The smoke from my cigarette on the table went up in a line that looked like it had been ruled with a straight-edge, the air was so still up here.

'I'd been gardening one afternoon,' the girl said. 'We had a lay-off at the studio. Some dispute among the electricians, I think. Anyway, I was home and I thought I'd put the south beds in order.'

She squinted at me against the sun. I must have had a strange expression for she suddenly smiled. It made the sunshine look quite faded.

'You're perfectly right, Mr Faraday,' she said. 'We do have an army of people to keep the grounds in shape. Only I happen to like gardening. And there are some things I prefer to do myself.'

I held my hand up with the fingers out.

'I didn't say a word,' I said.

The girl smiled again. She swept her hand out toward me, to embrace the whole façade of the Versailles palace behind us.

'You can see what sort of place it is. There are a lot of balconies with terraces. The house was a hotel at one time.'

The girl clasped both hands round her tall glass and frowned hard at it, like she was picking her words carefully.

'There are a number of big stone urns on the balconies. They're someone's idea of decor. They weigh about half a ton each. There wasn't a breath of wind that afternoon.'

'One of them fell?' I said.

The girl nodded. Her face had gone

suddenly white.

'I stepped back for some reason,' she said. 'The vase fell where I'd been a second or so before. It made a hole more than three feet deep in the soft earth.'

I didn't say anything for a moment.

'What else did you see?' I asked.

'The vase had come from the balcony running along in front of a small drawing room,' Candy Barr said. 'It's known as the Blue Room for some reason, though it's pale green nowadays. It's a sunny place where my husband and I like to write letters and read. I saw my husband dodge back from the edge of the balcony.'

I stopped writing and put another question.

'You're sure it was your husband?' I said.

'I didn't see his face properly, but it looked like Roy,' she said. 'He wore a brown suit and dark glasses. There's no one else around the place who fits that description.'

'So what did you do?' I asked.

'I beat it upstairs as fast as I could,' Candy Barr said. 'When I got to the Blue Room I found Roy there reading. He was wearing a brown suit and dark glasses so it must have been him.'

'Did you say anything?' I said.

The girl shook her head.

'I was pretty shaken. I didn't want to go into it all then. Roy seemed surprised to see me so I guessed he thought he'd succeeded in his aim.'

'It doesn't follow,' I said. 'Why would he stay around the room if he were guilty of something like that?'

'You don't know Roy,' the girl said. 'Besides, you haven't heard me out.'

'How far was the vase from where your husband was sitting?'

'About a hundred feet,' the girl said. 'He could have easily strolled back in the time.'

'There's something doesn't fit here,' I said. 'Does the balcony communicate with other rooms?'

'It runs along past three or four,' the girl said.

'What makes you so quick to give your husband the doubt?' I said.

There were little sparks dancing in Candy Barr's eyes.

'I'm insured in his favour for three million dollars,' she said.

CHAPTER SEVEN

I didn't say anything. There didn't seem anything to say. I sat and sipped my drink and admired the view and waited for the girl to continue. In the end the silence went on so long I turned to look at her. To my surprise she'd taken off the dark glasses and her eyes were brimming with tears. She got out a small lace handkerchief while I went on admiring the real estate.

'I'm sorry, Mr Faraday,' she said in a muffled voice when she'd recovered herself. 'I'm not usually like this. I've been under a strain lately.'

'It's all right,' I said. 'I understand. There must be more to it.'

'There is,' the girl said.

She took another sip of her long drink. She'd apparently recovered herself by now.

'I thought about the vase thing for several days. I didn't know what to do.'

'But you didn't tell anyone?' I said.

Candy Barr shook her head.

'I was stunned,' she said. 'Roy and I had been so close. Whatever way I twisted it around in my mind it always seemed to come out the same.'

I put down my glass and picked up my cigarette again. 'So you didn't want to believe,'

I said. 'That's understandable. What happened after that?'

The sound of the mower was louder now. I could see a monster scarlet machine eating up the lawn acreage below and coughing out the cuttings into a vast streamlined bin in rear. A man in a blue shirt and with a flaming mass of red hair sat up on the driver's seat and spun the wheel like he was on the race-track. I admired his straight lines for a minute or so before I turned back to the girl.

'I'd gone down to the studio one morning,' Candy Barr said. 'We were doing a difficult scene that took over a week to shoot. We needn't go into the details. They're too complicated.'

'Try me,' I said.

'It involved a fantasy sequence,' the girl said. 'I had to be suspended in a sort of leather harness on a wire against a black background. I had to mime and sing. Later the film would be combined with another so it looked like I was flying over an Eastern countryside.'

'This I've got to see,' I said.

The girl smiled wryly.

'You and me both,' she said. 'This is the film that's held up because of the union dispute. Where was I?'

'Up on the wire,' I said.

A shadow crossed the girl's face.

'I was up there over an hour that morning, sometimes forty feet from the ground. They'd just lowered me when the steel trace snapped. Thank God it hadn't happened a minute earlier.'

'A fault in the cable?' I said.

The girl shook her head.

'Naturally there was a full-scale studio inquiry. The technical people found a corrosive acid had been poured on to the wire. It had taken over an hour to eat through. Which is what saved me.'

I put my hand up and scratched my ear. The girl sat and watched me with an intent expression on her face.

'What do you say to that, Mr Faraday?'

'It's pretty convincing,' I said. 'Someone's out to get you. It certainly looks that way. But why blame your husband? Anyone at the studio could have played around with the cable.'

The girl tossed her blonde hair.

'Maybe,' she said. 'But Roy had come down to the studio that day. He was on set watching the takes. It was so rare as to be almost unique. I can only remember one other time he did that. And that was before we were married.'

I sat and watched my cigarette smoke ascending in the still, warm air.

'The studio hushed things up?' I said.

'What do you think?' the girl said.

'They gave it out that the cable had developed a minute flaw. Fortunately we'd finished the scenes. I don't think I could face going up again.'

'How many people knew about the real set-up?' I said.

Candy Barr smiled a thin smile.

'The studio people aren't fools,' she said. 'No-one got a sniff. It was a closed set anyway so there was only the camera crew and a handful of technicians. Brooker, the studio head knew the truth about the cable and a couple of people in the lab. Not more than about half a dozen in all.'

'What about your husband?' I said.

Before the girl could reply there was a snuffling noise and something crawled across my instep. I looked down to see the small wrinkled face I'd seen at the office. The miniature dog looked at me gravely, as though making up its mind. Apparently I didn't pass its scrutiny. It stepped daintily over my leg and scuttled under Candy Barr's chair. The girl picked the pooch up and crooned to it. The dog looked smugly across at me.

'Roy?' The girl frowned. 'He was concerned, naturally. He'd have to be in public. But he pretended to accept the official studio explanation.'

'Why "pretended"?' I said. 'He need not have been involved. Anyone at the studio could have tampered with the wire.'

The girl shook her head again.

'I haven't finished, Mr Faraday,' she said

58

impatiently. 'I'm coming to something conclusive.'

'It will have to be, Miss Barr,' I said. 'You haven't got anything yet that would stand up in a men's locker room, let alone in court.'

The girl's eyes flashed angrily at me but she didn't say anything for a minute. She turned back to look at the view below, her hands clasped round the stem of her long glass.

'I know it's difficult to convince an outsider,' she said at last. 'Look at it from my position.'

'I'm trying to,' I said. 'All I'm getting is a lot of possibilities. I admit your husband has the best of all motives. Three million motives, in fact. But according to all known facts he's a pretty wealthy character already. And surely your potential as a movie actress is worth a lot more than three million dollars. So why would he risk his neck for an insurance policy the company mightn't pay up on?'

The girl frowned like the notion hadn't occurred to her before.

'You have a point, Mr Faraday,' she said at last. 'I'm tired of kicking it around in my mind. That's what I'm going to pay you for. I'll just give you the facts and let you draw your own conclusions.'

'You mentioned something conclusive,' I said.

'It happened three days ago,' the girl said. 'Roy had just left to visit his office in L.A. He'd been down in the garage doing something to his car. He likes to tinker about down there. We have a chauffeur but Roy insists on doing all the work himself on his own cars. He's a qualified engineer and he has all the equipment.'

I nodded.

'What about the chauffeur?'

'It was Rogers' day off,' the girl said. 'Later that morning I intended to drive into L.A. myself. You won't know the lay-out, but the drive from the garage goes steeply down the hillside. We had some reconstruction work done and there's a rough-stone wall at the bottom; the drive bends fairly sharply past this. Roy had been gone about half an hour when I went down. I was using my white Mercedes that day.'

'Don't tell me the brakes failed?' I said.

The girl shot me a startled glance.

'How did you know?'

'It's old stuff,' I said. 'Besides, you were obviously leading up to it, with the details about the steep drive and the wall at the bottom.'

Candy Barr shifted her position on the cane lounging-chair and gave me a look in which I thought I could detect a tinge of fear.

'How I missed getting killed I'll never know,' she said. 'I rolled out and the brakes gave even before I could get the car in gear. I just managed to swerve round the wall, but I tore the wing off the car.'

60

I didn't say anything for a minute. Like the girl said, things were building up against her husband. But it was far too early to jump to any conclusions.

'You had the car checked?' I said.

'I had it towed to the studio,' the girl said. 'Their technical people went over it in confidence. It was the same corrosive on the brake cables that was used on the trace in the studio scene.'

'And your husband was the only person around the garage that day, Miss Barr,' I said. 'I admit it fits. And you were right to be scared. Why didn't the studio call the police in?'

The girl shook her head. 'Too much scandal,' she said. 'Brooker wouldn't risk it. He recommended you. I must say I think he made the right choice. They thought you could look out for me. They're going to take special precautions while I'm on the lot.'

'All right, Miss Barr,' I said. 'You've given me the picture. Now I'll want the answers to a few questions.'

'Anything,' Candy Barr said.

'Your car,' I said. 'How would your husband have known you'd use the Mercedes? You've got more than one, I take it?'

The girl smiled like she could read my thoughts.

'My other personal car was at the studio,' she said. 'Rogers had the Studebaker. We let him drive it on his days off.' There was only the Mercedes and Roy's Maserati. He'd never let me drive that and I wouldn't want to, anyway. It's far too powerful and dangerous for me.'

I made another note on the pad.

'I can't do the bodyguard stuff,' I said. 'It isn't my line.'

The girl shook her head. The sunlight caught her dark glasses, reflecting blinding flashes off the rims.

'I know that, Mr Faraday,' she said gently. 'I didn't hire you for that. I want you to sniff around and see what you can find out. Specially while Roy's not here.'

'That's not good reasoning, Miss Barr,' I said. 'Firstly, I'd rather have your husband around. He might give something away. He's not likely to have left anything on the estate which might implicate him in an attempt on your life. Secondly, your security precautions at the gate are going to make it pretty tough for me to come and go.'

'I can't do anything about Roy being away,' Candy Barr said. 'You'll have to do the best you can. At least you can look around the house without arousing his suspicions. As to the second thing, we have another entrance. It's on a private road about a mile down. An electronically controlled steel shutter comes down across the drive. You operate it with a special magnetic key.'

I looked at the girl for a long moment.

'You want to know how many keys there are?' she said. 'The servants go out the front way. There's only Roy and myself and Paul Sheridan hold keys.'

'Who's he?' I said.

'My personal manager,' the girl said. 'You'll like Paul. Everyone does. He's been with me ten years. He created me, really.'

'And he gets ten per cent of everything,' I said. 'Nice for him.'

Candy Barr grinned. It lit her whole face up and gave it a sweetness that mere beauty couldn't have achieved. I could see now why she had made it to the top in the movies.

'You're too cynical, Mr Faraday,' she said. 'It was nice for me too. I wouldn't have got where I am if it hadn't been for Paul.'

She reached under the table again and rummaged around in her bag.

'Here's my key. I can get another out of my bank deposit box tomorrow.'

She slid the flat piece of triangular metal over to me. It had a small hole punched in it. I took it from her and put it on my own key chain.

'Don't lose it,' she said.

I shook my head.

'You're talking to the brain of Einstein in the body of John Wayne, remember?' I said. 'I'm not the sort of character who would lose a key. You said so yourself.'

The girl uncurled herself from the chair, all her worries momentarily erased from her face. The little dog whimpered as he floundered on her lap. Then she picked him up and held him to the front of her jacket. I got up and finished my drink. I looked at my watch. It was already five-thirty. The girl misinterpreted my action.

'There's no need to go, Mr Faraday,' she said. 'We eat at six-thirty, if you'd care to stay on.'

'That would be fine,' I said. 'Right now I'd like to have a look around.'

'Surely,' Candy Barr said. 'We'll go on up to the house.'

We walked back along the terrace, between the statuary and the fountains, the dog looking at me with its little prejudiced eyes, our feet clicking hollowly on the flagstones. A scent of mimosa was coming from somewhere which made me remember things which happened a long time ago.

'How are you going to explain my presence to your husband?' I said.

'We'll think of something,' the girl said calmly. 'You could have come out to do an inventory of the paintings or books.'

'I've had that before,' I said. 'He'd soon trip me up if he knows anything about art. I couldn't tell a Monet from a Manet.'

'You've heard of Monet, anyway,' the girl said coolly. 'How many people in California could say that.'

We were nearly up to the chateau now, its bulk climbing steadily up the sky until it dwarfed everything. It made Hearst's place at San Simeon look like a phone booth.

A low burbling roar cut across the distant clatter of the mower. The sleek scarlet bulk of a roadster slid across the pink gravel of the driveway at the end of the lawn. A tall figure at the wheel waved to the girl.

'That's Paul now,' the girl said. 'I'd like you to meet him.'

CHAPTER EIGHT

The man who advanced across the grass to meet us was tall and blond. He wore a green-flecked hounds-tooth jacket and drill trousers with blue canvas sneakers. On anyone else the rig-out would have looked incongruous. On him it looked good.

He walked with easy, rangy movements and though he must have been over forty he had the look of an athlete about him. As he got up closer I could see he had a square jaw, a humorous mouth. His strong white teeth were clamped over the stem of a Meerschaum pipe and blue clouds of fragrantly perfumed smoke followed him across the gardens. His eyes were grey and were appraising me carefully as he came. He looked like a shrewd character; but then I guessed he'd have to be if he looked after Candy Barr's business affairs and contracts.

He greeted the girl informally and with affection and waited diffidently to be introduced. His handclasp was firm and incisive. He had a personality it was hard to dislike. I wondered how the girl would introduce me. I wasn't disappointed.

'This is Mr Faraday, Paul,' she said. 'He'll be staying on for a meal with us.'

'Fine, Candy,' Sheridan said. 'We'd better

talk business now, in that case. Mr Faraday won't want to be bored at supper.'

He grinned at me.

'That's all right, Paul,' the girl said. 'If you've got the contracts I can sign them now. Mr Faraday was going to have a look around the property, anyway.'

'Thinking of buying the place, Mr Faraday?'

Sheridan grinned again. His smile was quite disarming so it was difficult to take offence. Not that I would have.

'It's a little out of my price-range, Mr Sheridan,' I said.

'Mr Faraday's going to run over the inventory, Paul,' the girl said. 'I'm thinking of having the house and contents reinsured.'

'Great,' Sheridan said.

He looked quizzically at me. The girl had her dark cheaters on again so I couldn't read her expression.

'You can't be too careful these days. I'll see you later, then.'

He excused himself and strolled over onto the terrace. The girl took my arm and steered me up toward the house.

'You aren't letting him in on it?' I said.

Candy Barr shook her head.

'But nobody,' she said. 'This is between you and me and your secretary. That way we'll get somewhere.'

'And Brooker,' I reminded her.

'He's like a clam,' she said. 'He

recommended you, remember?'

'That's all right, then,' I said. 'Just the four of us. Where do I start?'

The girl stood on one leg and scratched her scarlet-clad instep with the back of the other. She surveyed me silently. The little dog sneered. Out on the terrace Sheridan was studying the view. I could read the impatience in the immobile set of his back.

'You've got the whole run of the house and grounds, Mr Faraday,' the girl said. 'That means what it says. If there's anything special you want to see, just ask Rita. See you in an hour.'

She turned away and ran down toward Sheridan. I went on up toward the house. I didn't waste any time examining the Maserati. It would only have spoilt my afternoon. I worked my way around the house. The sound of mowing went on in the distance but I couldn't see anyone about. The place was even bigger than I figured. It took me about half an hour to make a complete circle. I got to the front again. The girl and Sheridan had disappeared from the terrace now. I stood frowning at the façade.

I walked over in among the beds which flanked the frontage of the mansion. It didn't take me long to find what I was looking for. There was a big indentation in the soft ground. Like the girl said it was all of three feet deep. They must have used a fork-lift to get the urn out. I looked up at the balustrade. There was a gap between the other two vases. Even from here I could see it was impossible for it to have fallen accidentally. I found the urn itself, still crusted with earth, leaning against the bottom of a flight of steps a few moments later.

I went on up the steps. There was a big orangery set against the façade here. I opened the white-painted lattice doors and stepped through. It was moist and green in here and the decaying smell of tropical plants came with a cloying sickness to my nostrils. It was the smell of over-ripeness; success turned in on itself and corrupted. Like Hollywood itself. I grinned, stepping along the dim, leafy aisles. I was beginning to sound like a Hollywood cliché myself.

I went in through the orangery and found myself in a fantastic room about sixty feet long, decorated in rococo style. I went out in the hall. That was marble-floored and a flight of jumbo jets could have landed there without disturbing the decor. I went up the curving marble staircase without being stopped by anyone. I wanted the room on to which the balcony gave. I didn't expect to find anything, but at least I could satisfy myself about what hadn't happened the day the urn almost blotted out one of the cinema's brightest stars.

I found it in the end. It was like the girl said. I could see where the husband had sat. I walked on over to the balcony. The big double doors leading to the room were slid back and I stood on the tiling for a minute or two, the heat of the sun coming up like burnished metal from the stones of the balcony and the tiles.

From this height I could see there was an ornamental lake in the far distance. I lit a cigarette and stood and looked at the spot where the urn had stood. There was nothing but a flat, circular shape in the stone of the broad-topped balcony, the surface crushed and friable with the weight. I went over to the next in the line. I put all my weight and strength against it. It rocked a little on the balcony. With a terrific effort I could have toppled it. But it couldn't have fallen accidentally, that was for sure.

I stood and finished my cigarette and watched the lake. There was a splash of scarlet along the far shore. Candy Barr and her manager were walking round, discussing contracts and percentages no doubt. I frowned. It's another world, Faraday, I told myself.

I walked on down the balcony. I found there were two other rooms which gave on to it. I went back into the big room. I sat down on the divan. From where Roy Lawrence had been sitting he couldn't have seen the terrace or the ornamental vases. The divan faced away from the window. That might or might not be important. I finished my cigarette and stubbed it out in a jade ashtray.

2

I was still sitting there when the maid Rita passed though from the landing outside. She was still the only servant I'd seen. For an establishment the size Candy Barr was running they seemed pretty thin on the ground. Unless she'd sent them away for my visit. The girl in the blue outfit paused and fiddled with a vase of flowers near the French doors. She gave me an enigmatic smile.

'Is there anything I can do for you, Mr Faraday?' she said in the huskiest voice I'd heard this side of Eartha Kitt.

I shook my head.

'I'm just fine, thanks,' I said.

The girl hovered for a minute or two longer.

'If there's anything you need, I'll be in the kitchen,' she said.

She pointed to a marble-topped table near the divan.

'There's a button on the phone marked Kitchen. You can reach me from any floor.'

There was an odd expression at the back of her eyes I couldn't read. I thanked her and she went on out. I sat and admired her walk all the way to the door. Then I jerked my gaze away and got back to business. It was too hot for that sort of thing this afternoon. I grinned to myself. It always was around L.A.

I got tired of the Blue Room after a bit. I

wandered over to the balcony but Candy Barr and her companion had disappeared into the vastness of the grounds. I glanced at my watch. I still had a bit of time in hand. I went back downstairs again and through the orangery into the open air. I walked around the house. I was making for the garage this time. This was a long, low block, more recent than the main house and separated from it by a high, flowering hedge.

I walked through an archway cut in the hedge and studied the lay-out. I wanted to make sure the chauffeur wasn't around. It would only arouse suspicion if I were seen poking about there. And if he were involved it would tip my hand straight away. I stood for a minute or two enjoying the sunshine, the clear air and the perfume of flowers from the garden. I couldn't hear anything and there didn't seem to be anyone around. I guessed Candy Barr would have sent him off somewhere too.

When I was sure the garage block was empty I walked on over. The drive was floored with pink tarmac and there was a big half-moon area in front of the sectional doors. I looked inside the building. There were two vehicles still in but the place was so big it could have held eight cars with ease. I walked back into the centre of the crescent. There were stainless steel drains here where the cars would be washed. There was plenty of room to turn.

I soon saw why. Because of the configuration of the land here, they'd had to narrow the driveway considerably. Like Candy Barr said it went straight down at a very steep angle. A shoulder of hill, which looked mostly solid rock, reared up at the end. The drive curved and went around a buttress. I couldn't see much from the top, except a long, steep green tunnel stippled with sunlight. It would be an ideal place for the sort of accident Candy Barr had described.

I went on down. The grade was so steep I had to walk on my heels. It was steeper if anything as it neared the shoulder of granite. I stood and studied the entrance where the drive curved round the hill at the end. They'd constructed a rough stone wall to give an ornamental effect to the rock face. If they'd wanted to excavate and make the drive any wider they'd have to have shifted tons of rock because the cliff was about forty feet thick at this point.

There was some oil on the drive and I soon saw where three or four big stones had been torn out the wall at its very edge. I didn't hang around long. There wasn't much else to see and I didn't want anyone on the grounds staff to become curious at my activities. I walked back up to the garage again. If anyone had been meddling around with corrosives there might be something there. I couldn't go to the studio, that was for sure. With a dead end there the only other place would be the garage. And I'd have to give Lawrence's bedroom the once-over later.

I'd need the girl for that. She'd have to make sure no-one was around while I went through his things. I frowned at the sunlit circle of tarmac. There were a number of unpleasant aspects to this case. And it hadn't even begun yet. There didn't seem much percentage in admiring the climate so I went on into the garage. There was benching at the back and a series of shelves which might yield something. There was another door in rear which presumably led to the house. I went over and turned the key in the lock. Then I came back and went down the benches.

I didn't know what I was looking for. Whatever it was I didn't find it. I found a big pool of oil in one corner. In fact there were several pools scattered about, presumably where the family's various cars were parked. Someone had put sheets of newspaper down to catch the drips. The girl had told me where the Mercedes usually stood so I concentrated on that.

There was no newspaper in that area. Someone might have removed it because it had become too soaked. But in that case why hadn't the paper been replaced? The Barr household evidently cared enough to prevent oil from reaching the concrete floor. Or had someone removed the paper because it contained traces of some powerful acid which had dripped down from the brake cables?

That was a more interesting line. There was a garbage bin in a corner and I poked around in that for a bit, not really expecting to come up with anything. If I was hoping to find a few sheets of oil-stained newspaper crumpled into a ball I didn't get them. That would have been too easy. And it's never easy in my racket. I sighed. There was nothing on the floor of the bin but a cardboard carton which had once contained sparkplugs. I replaced the plastic lid and went back into the middle of the floor.

It was then I became aware I wasn't alone. There was a long shadow stencilled across the concrete ramp in front of me. For a moment I thought it might have been cast by the sun striking against a post. But then I saw it was a human figure. I didn't know how long it had been there but someone must have been watching me. Whoever he or she was must have been standing in the doorway cut into the flowering hedge, looking directly toward the garage.

I couldn't see the watcher because he was cut off by the inside garage wall. He was standing exactly where I'd stood myself a few minutes earlier. I moved over toward the garage entrance when the shadow seemed to flicker and disappear. I pounded across the sunlit crescent of pink tarmac. I knew what had happened. The scrape of my foot had carried and the watcher at the hedge had simply stepped sideways.

Like I figured there was no-one around when I got to the spot. I found a toe-print of a man's shoe in the soft earth of a flower-bed a few yards farther on. Then the grounds doubled round between hedged walks and through flowering shrubbery. He could have played hide-and-seek with me out there for hours without me spotting him. I grinned and walked back down toward the terrace. Things were becoming decidedly more interesting.

CHAPTER NINE

1

I heard Candy Barr calling then. I went down to join her. She still wore the glasses and her face was flushed with sun and wind. She put her hand impulsively through my arm and walked with me along to the orangery entrance.

'How did you make out?' she said.

'I had a look around,' I said. 'The Blue Room, the garage, the drive.'

The girl took off her dark cheaters with her disengaged hand. Her eyes were very brown and very worried as she searched my face.

'And?'

I smiled.

'Too early to tell,' I said. 'It could mean anything or nothing. It's too soon to say.'

'But you see Roy had every opportunity,' the girl persisted. 'And he had everything to gain.'

'We'll see,' I said gently. 'Best to take it as it comes.'

I looked around the terrace. We were almost up to the orangery now. The scarlet roadster still stood shimmering in the late afternoon sunlight.

'Where's Sheridan?' I said.

'Gone to wash up,' the girl said. 'He'll be joining us shortly. I thought it would be a good opportunity to talk.'

'It would be if we had anything to talk about,' I said.

I followed the girl in through the orangery and into the gigantic rococo room; lights burned softly in wall sconces now. There was a massive bay window up at one end with a view of haze and distant blue mountains. A vast circular dining table was set in the bay. The lamplight glittered on silver and crystal. There were two or three trolleys on the carpet a short distance from the table which was laid for three. Two Filipinos in short white jackets stood and talked quietly to themselves by the trolleys, their patent-leather hair gleaming under the lamps. The girl in blue shirt and slacks waited patiently near the window.

'I expect you'd like to wash up too, Mr Faraday,' Candy Barr said. 'Rita will show you the way.'

The girl came gliding down the room as she caught Candy Barr's eye. She seemed alive to the slightest nuance or gesture of her mistress. I admired her sinuous back all the way up the grand staircase.

'Have you been with Miss Barr long, Rita?' I said.

The girl smiled hesitantly over her shoulder.

'More than three years now, Mr Faraday. Best position I ever had.'

'I can well imagine,' I said. 'You know everything going on around here?

The girl stopped on the landing and faced me squarely.

'Miss Barr trusts me implicitly,' she said. 'There is something phoney going on. Is that why you're here?'

I shook my head.

'Just curious, Rita. I might want your help, that's all.'

The girl continued to regard me in the same level way.

'I think I can trust you, Mr Faraday,' she said. 'I can't talk now.'

'I'll be back,' I said. 'There'll be opportunities. You hinted things weren't right. What sort of things?'

The girl hesitated. She'd just opened her mouth to speak when a door slammed in the far distance. Her attitude changed.

'First on the right at the end of the corridor, Mr Faraday,' she said in a loud voice.

Paul Sheridan was coming down the passageway whistling a jaunty tune. He was so effortlessly turned out he looked like a character from a thirties movie comedy. I always envy guys who can take a bundle of old clothes and make a fashion-plate out of them. Expensive old clothes, of course. Whatever the gift was Sheridan certainly had it.

He smiled as he got level with me.

'Out of soap again,' he said cheerily.

He winked at me.

'You'll have to get with it, Rita.'

'Someone steals it,' the coffee-coloured girl said calmly. 'I'm thinking of installing one of those liquid soap machines like they have in public lavatories.'

Sheridan gurgled with laughter like the idea appealed to him.

'How would you know, Rita?' he said. 'I thought they only had that kind in men's toilets.'

The girl turned pink.

'I got my informants,' she said.

I went on along the corridor as the girl turned back down the staircase. I could hear Sheridan descending three at a time. I guessed he'd just cut himself another expensive piece of property on the deals he'd been discussing on the walk round the lake. I sighed. It seemed more of an unequal world than ever.

2

It was long after dark when I left. The dinner had been as good as I'd have expected of someone with Candy Barr's money and taste. Sheridan had been entertaining company too. We hadn't touched on the reason for my presence at the house. Sheridan didn't exactly strike me as being the over-curious type. He and the girl were too busy trying to score professional points off each other. I just sat and shovelled food into my mouth and listened to the wisecracks. It was the sort of world I didn't get in on very often and I was making the most of it.

Sheridan was the first to leave. He gunned his Maserati down the private drive a little after nine. He leaned out the door to shake hands. There was a slight wind now, probing nervously in the roots of his blond hair.

'I like you, Faraday,' he said. 'Look me up any time you're passing the office.'

'Sure,' I said.

He knew he'd never be seeing me again unless it was at Candy Barr's place. And I knew I'd never look by his office. It was just one of those things people said after a pleasant evening when drink had loosened their tongues. But I didn't think any the worse of him for it. He grinned. He knew I knew it was just small talk. We watched his tail light out of sight down the road before we moved over to the Buick.

'When will I be seeing you again, Mr Faraday?' the girl said.

She'd put on a white fur wrap like the weather was cold tonight and she shrugged it more tightly around her.

'I'll try and look by tomorrow,' I said. 'I'll ring in, just in case you're at the studio.'

'Come on out, anyway,' the girl said. 'The staff have their instructions. You're allowed free access. You haven't been over Roy's room yet.'

'I'd better wait until you're there,' I said. 'I'll keep probing, don't worry.'

'I'm not worried, Mr Faraday,' the girl said. 'Don't forget, just put the magnetic key in the tray.'

'I'll remember,' I said.

The girl came over impulsively toward me. She kissed me solemnly on the forehead, her perfume heady in my nostrils. Then she pushed away and was running back across the tarmac and up the steps, her blonde hair flying in the wind. I stood and watched her go, still feeling the touch of her moist lips on my skin. I could see the tall form of Rita, the coloured girl, silhouetted against the warm glow of the terrace lamps. I got in the Buick with all sorts of thoughts chasing themselves around in my mind.

I gunned the car out, the headlamps stencilling yellow beams of light across the private road in front of me. It seemed to stretch on for miles, winding back on itself, until I'd lost my sense of direction. Then there were red lights coming at me out of the dark. I saw then they were glass reflectors studded all over the surface of a massive steel fence that blocked off the road from the outside world. There was a grey-painted pillar at one side of the road with a faint light coming from it.

I got out the car and went on over. The illumination came from a strip light set above a scanning tray. White letters on black said: Danger—Gate will remain up for 15 seconds only before descending. I went back to the Buick and started the engine again. I got out the flat piece of metal the girl had given me and laid it down in the tray. There was a short delay and then a faint whining noise. Arc-lights suddenly came on and the metal barrier went creaking upwards. I already had the key in my pocket and was climbing behind the wheel. I didn't aim to hang around.

I rolled the Buick forward and stopped. I waited until the gate had slid down behind me. It fitted into a steel groove in the roadway. The thing was about 20 feet high with thick barbed wire on top. It looked pretty thief-proof to me. There were arc-lights on this side of the gate too, and another metal post with a key-tray. The private road wound on before me. I put the car in gear and drove on back to the main stem.

I saw the lights of the traffic long before I got to it. I saw something else too. Just before the private road hit the major route there was a car stalled on the verge. It had its headlights on and the bonnet was up. There was a man with his head stuck inside the engine and another standing beside the car. I reached inside my jacket and broke out the Smith-Wesson. I eased off the safety and laid the gun down on the seat at my side. I don't know why I did this but there was something not quite right about the set-up.

No-one but myself and Sheridan should have been on the private road. If these two characters had broken down why hadn't they asked for help from passing drivers on the major route? I knew the answer anyway. I'd been around too long. They were waiting for me. I picked up the Smith-Wesson with my left hand and held it on the lower rim of the steering wheel as I glided slowly toward the stalled auto. The bigger of the two men was coming forward into the road now. He held up his hand, an ingratiating smile on his face. I smiled to myself. That was the standard opening too.

The man who beckoned me to a halt wore a dark, anonymous-looking suit with a white shirt and discreet tie with a mottled pattern. He had heavy muscling over the shoulders and the way his jacket bulged over his heavy frame, the material stretched taut, proved he was a solid customer. I decided to deal with him first. He was about forty and had a broad, flat face with wide, expressionless eyes. I could see that much in the beam from the Buick's headlights as I glided toward him.

The pug's arms were long and hung down slackly at his sides like a gorilla. He wore a dark grey homburg hat that sat incongruously on his thick skull so I couldn't see the colour of his hair. I fancied there was a deep scar running from the corner of his mouth and up across his cheek. I looked around for Boris Karloff but the other man didn't fit the picture. He'd be the wheelman. He was short and pudgy and I could see from the way he was bent forward over the engine of the car that he was only fooling around and not doing anything to the engine. Anything important, that is.

The second man wore a dark suit too and as he kept his back turned I didn't get to see his face for a minute. I was still a yard or two away from the big man when he spoke.

'Having a little trouble,' he said.

He was still smiling so I guess he thought he was on an easy assignment. He had a flat, metallic voice to match his face. I saw something glitter in his right hand then. It was a piece of wire like they use for slicing cheese in the delicatessens. Only these mugs didn't use them for slicing cheese. I could see the big man was wearing gloves now. That was to save his hands if they slipped off the wooden handles.

'Too bad,' I said.

I accelerated up suddenly when I was only a couple of feet away. The snout of the Buick leapt forward. I heard the second man shout and the big man's smile changed to an expression of alarm. The bodywork of the Buick slammed him back. He'd been caught off balance and he went down, landing awkwardly on his back. I could have gunned out but I was curious by this time. I put on the brake and turned off the ignition almost in one.

I vaulted over the driving door as the big man started to get up. His face was white with pain so I guessed he might have sprained something. I hoped so anyway. I had the Smith-Wesson in my right and I chopped with the barrel at the big man's head. He ducked but he wasn't quite quick enough and the steel raked along his neck. He grunted and fell forward on to his knees. Blood gleamed redly on the side of his face.

I didn't have time to see what the second man was doing. Now I was up close I could see the character with the cheese-cutter was as big as a house. He sat on his haunches and shook his head to clear it, while his two hands fumbled painfully together to fashion the wire into a noose. I knew I'd never make it if I let him up. I kicked him in the stomach as I moved around him. I put a lot of weight behind it.

The big man sagged forward, the air whistling out of his lungs. I hit him with all the force I could muster while he was still going forward. I felt the vibration all the way along the metal of the gun. The barrel made a dull cracking noise as it connected with the bone behind his ear. All the intelligence went out of the big man's eyes. What there was of it, anyway. He pitched forward onto his face and lay still. The wire noose fell from his hand and I kicked it away, out of the headlights.

All this had taken perhaps five seconds. The other man had been a spectator too long. He was still reaching in his inside pocket when I came around the sedan in a tearing rush. I pulled out the bonnet retainer with my shoulder. The fat man screamed as the bonnet came down on his hand. He doubled over in agony. I reached in his pocket and took the fat cannon from him. I jammed the Smith-Wesson hard in against his gut. As hard in as his trembling would let me.

'Just take it nice and easy, fatty,' I said. 'And no-one will get hurt.'

I pulled the pudgy man back clear of his stalled car and dragged him over toward the muscle man. He was still sprawled on his face and I could tell by the gargling noise he was making through his nose he'd be out some time.

I made the fat man stand with his two hands over the Buick's driving door while I ran through the big man's pockets. I didn't find anything. He was clean. I guessed he relied on his hands and the cheese-cutter. He wouldn't need anything else. I went back over to the fat man. I jabbed the Smith-Wesson up against the side of his head.

He licked his lips and his little eyes searched my face.

'Now we get to talk,' I said.

CHAPTER TEN

The pudgy man's face was creased with pain. I could see his right hand now. It was thickly caked with blood and a small globule of red ran off the edge of his thumb. I reached in his pocket and pulled out his handkerchief.

'Wrap that around it,' I said. 'But no funny stuff.'

The handkerchief fell to the ground. I stepped back and watched the fat boy carefully while he stooped for it. He grunted with pain as he tightened the improvised bandage round his injured hand. When he'd finished I made him put his hands back in the same position. I glanced over at the big man on the ground. The distant traffic went by with a slurring of tyres in the hot night.

The beams of the headlights didn't reach this far back so I knew we wouldn't be disturbed. I figured the chill merchant would be out for a good half hour, probably a lot longer. I had as much time as I needed. I went and stood by the fat man. He'd recovered himself a little by now and gazed stonily ahead. I figured he was probably as durable as his partner. I'd soon find out. The wheelman wore another anonymous dark suit and a conservative sort of tie.

He had long black hair that fell over his

collar. His face was inflamed with sun and wind and his tiny blue eyes were almost lost in folds of skin. But he had a hard, square jaw and his fleshy lips were locked in a sullen expression like he was used to being worked over.

'Now you're comfortable we can get down to business,' I said.

'What business?' he said.

He had a flat, metallic voice to match that of his partner. His teeth were very white in the pinkness of his face.

'You ought to know,' I said. 'You were the ones who tried to shake me down.'

The pudgy man put up one hand as if to gesticulate.

'What you talking about?' he said thickly.

'Just keep your hands on the car door,' I said. 'I get rather nervous.'

'We was having trouble with the car,' the fat man said in the same stolid voice. 'We wanted help.'

'Like hell you did,' I said.

I jerked the Smith-Wesson barrel over toward the figure of the big man on the ground.

'I suppose you wanted me to tow you into town,' I said. 'With a nice comfortable wire noose around my neck? Try some other story, sonny.'

The fat man scowled.

'I still say you got it all wrong,' he said. 'Why

should we want to shake you down?'

'You tell me,' I said. 'Only I haven't got much time and my trigger finger is liable to get a little nervous this time of night.'

The fat man clenched his pudgy knuckles over the top of the car door. He shrugged. His heavy face looked like he was having a hard struggle thinking up something plausible.

'Like I said we had a cylinder missing on the car,' he said.

He groaned with pain as I brought the Smith-Wesson barrel down on the knuckles of his left, uninjured hand. He bent over so far I thought he was going to knock his head on the windscreen. I moved the barrel around and watched him carefully.

'I don't hear you so good,' I said. 'And I can't bear to be around liars.'

The fat man didn't say anything for a minute. He put his left hand under his right armpit and rocked to and fro, nursing his fingers.

'Now you got the set,' I said. 'Put them back on the door.'

Sweat ran down the fat man's face. He slowly straightened up. He put his hands back on the door, looking at me apprehensively.

'You work around Belsen, mister, on your days off,' he said hoarsely.

Strangely, I rather liked him at that moment. He had a certain quality of stoicism about him.

'I'm only rough to people I don't know very well,' I said. 'You'll like me better when you know me. Besides, I haven't forgotten the cheese-cutter yet. It took away all my natural kindness.'

'I'll bet,' the fat man said, between clenched teeth. He stared stolidly in front of him, half-flinching at the prospect of the next blow.

'Save yourself some grief,' I advised him. 'Come clean.'

The fat man shrugged again.

'About what?' he said.

'Who sent you to rub me?' I said. 'It's been tried before recently. It can't be coincidence.'

'I don't know what you're talking about,' the fat man said. 'Like I said . . .'

'If you repeat that story about the car I shall scream,' I told him. 'I want the name of the man who sent you and why.'

The fat man turned to face me. The pain still lingered around the eyes but his voice was steady enough.

'You want a lot, mister,' he said.

He sighed heavily.

'You want for me to finish up in an alley full of airholes and no breath.'

It was my turn to shrug.

'We got to do it the hard way then, fats,' I said. 'This just isn't your night.'

I swung the Smith-Wesson again. The fat man tried to move his hand but he was too late. It was only a tap this time but on top of the first blow it made him howl. Tears ran out the corners of his eyes. He looked at the night sky like he was praying.

'He won't help you,' I said. 'You're dealing with me tonight.'

The fat man swore solidly for a whole minute. While he was doing that I moved around him, going over his pockets. There was only money, car keys, a few other things like a pipe and a tobacco pouch. No wallet, no letters or documents. Nothing that would identify him. Like I figured these boys were professionals. I waited until the fat man had finished his recital. I went to stand over by the big man on the ground.

'You won't find anything,' the wheelman said. 'He's clean too.'

'I can believe it,' I said.

I went back over toward him. He straightened his back and leaned forward against the Buick again. The big cannon I'd taken from him felt hard and heavy in my right-hand pocket.

'I don't like this any more than you do,' I said.

'You want to put that in writing?' the fat man said.

I looked at him closely. He held both hands over the edge of the Buick door like it was red-hot. His eyes were half-closed, waiting for the next blow.

'You can relax,' I said. 'No more rough stuff.

If we spend much more time together I shall end up liking you.'

'I handle the public relations end,' the fat man said. 'My partner takes care of the fist work. You wouldn't like him at all.'

'You got me convinced,' I said.

The fat man blinked at me. A tear ran out the corner of his right eye and traced a shiny mark down his cheek.

'I could use a cigarette,' he said.

I got out my pack and fit one for him. I put it in the corner of his mouth. He inhaled the smoke gratefully. I watched him carefully all the time but he didn't make any attempt to shift his hands from the door.

'You're all right, mister,' he said.

'When I'm decently treated,' I said. 'How about it?'

The fat man shrugged.

'No harm in telling you,' he said. 'We're from out of town. Hired for the job.'

I looked from him to the motionless form of the big man. The distant lights of the cars stippled alternate bars of yellow and black across the dusty road.

'Who put the finger on me?' I said.

The fat man shook his head. He held up one placatory hand. I gestured my permission with the Smith-Wesson barrel. The wheelman took the cigarette out of his mouth and removed a flake of tobacco from the corner of his lips with a blue tongue. He shrugged again.

'You know how these things are done,' he said. 'We just got a phone call. We pick up half the notes and details of the hit. We get the other half by mail when we get back.'

'Honour among thieves,' I said. 'Go on.'

The fat man put the cigarette back in his mouth again. His voice was low and stoical, like he'd been all through this before. He adjusted the handkerchief around his hand and then put both hands back up on top of the car door. He smiled a slow smile.

'You know the system better than that, mister,' he said. 'Nothing else to tell. An anonymous voice made the arrangements. We watch the booth. An anonymous guy leaves the parcel. No ends that way.'

'What sort of anonymous guy?' I said.

The fat man crinkled up his eyes like the smoke from his cigarette was hurting him.

'A tall guy in a dark hat and a white belted raincoat,' he said.

'That shouldn't fit more than half a million characters in the city,' I said. 'Any more useful information like that?'

The fat man chuckled.

'We're pro's, mister. Like you. That's how we operate.'

'You weren't very professional about this,' I said. 'You'd better get on out before they ask for their deposit back.'

The wheelman scowled suddenly, erasing the smile.

'Yeah, we didn't do so well,' he admitted. 'Some contracts go by the book. Others ain't so smooth. This is one of the rough ones.'

He looked at me warily, cocking his head over one shoulder. I had his gun open, breaking out the shells. I put the empty pistol back in his pants pocket.

'This mean we're free to go?' he said.

'Why not?' I said. 'You'll just about make the nine o'clock plane from L.A. International.'

The fat man took down his hands from the car door and rubbed his jaw wearily.

'How do you know that's the plane we want?' he said.

'You got it stamped all over you,' I said. 'And if you do run across the guy who booked you tell him I don't shove around so easy.'

The fat man looked at me thoughtfully. He lowered his hands from the door and fingered the one with the bandage gingerly. He went over to the big man on the ground. He took him under the arm-pits and started dragging him back toward the sedan. I kept the Smith-Wesson in my hand and took the big man's legs. We got him into the rear seat of the other car. Blood was trickling out his nose by now. The fat man slammed the rear door and stood looking at me questioningly.

'This your wagon?' I said.

He shook his head.

'What do you take me for? Hired for the

day.'

'You'd better get it fixed and hop off,' I said.

The fat man grinned. He went around the bonnet and slammed it shut. He came back and slid behind the wheel. He looked at me with grudging respect.

'I can't say it's been a pleasure,' he said. 'More like an experience.'

He gunned out with a squealing of tyres. I stood and watched him until his headlights merged with the traffic stream on the major road. When he'd disappeared I went over to the Buick and cut the main beam.

I saw something white glimmering on the ground then. It was a small piece of pasteboard. It had been right where the fat boy had been standing. It must have fallen from his pocket when I pulled the handkerchief out. I picked it up. I took it over under the sidelight to look at.

It was one of those cards hotels and guest houses use to advertise their services and telephone numbers. It said: Rainbow Lake Hunting Lodge in curlicue script. There were some more details in smaller type underneath. I put the card back in my pocket. Looked like the professionals were slipping tonight.

I got behind the wheel and put the Smith-Wesson away. I lit a cigarette and put the spent match in the dashboard tray. I sat feathering smoke at the stars and trying to figure out the score. I didn't get very far. I gave it up in the end and drove back into L.A.

CHAPTER ELEVEN

1

'Are you the model for the new statue on Berkeley Campus or just thinking?' Stella said.

I uncoiled my feet from off my broadtop and took my hand down from my chin.

'It's what's called a brown study, Watson,' I said.

'You could have fooled me,' Stella said darkly.

She went over to her own desk and put down a bundle of magazines and a jazzy-looking red leather handbag.

'If I didn't know you better I might take offence at that,' I said.

'That'll be the day,' Stella said.

She went over to the glassed-in alcove where we brewed the coffee and fussed about. I heard the welcome clink of cups and saucers. Stella looked great today. She had on a brown silk trouser suit that made her body undulate every time she moved. Or it may have been the other way around. I couldn't make up my mind. It was a fascinating problem. I could have studied it for hours. The lights shone on the gold bell of her hair as she clicked across the floor back to her own desk.

'O what are the wild waves saying?' I said.

Stella smiled. I could see she'd got the message all right.

'I thought you hadn't noticed,' she said.

'Lame and old and arthritic I may be but blind I'm not,' I said.

Stella smiled again. She went back to the alcove and did something mysterious with cups and saucers.

'A friend was passing through Dallas last week,' she said. 'She called in at Niemann Marcus for me.'

'If this is mail-order I'm for it,' I said.

Stella sighed like I'd slipped a cog.

'You're not very bright this afternoon,' she said.

'I'm never very bright any afternoon,' I said.

Stella ignored that. She came back and put the brew down on my blotter in front of me.

'I went up to Dallas last month on a long week-end, remember,' she said. 'I bought the outfit then. They had to make some alterations for me.'

'Bully for them,' I said. 'Remind me to send you up to Dallas again.'

I stirred my cup and blinked at the tin Stella had put down with it.

'I got a new selection of biscuits,' Stella said. 'Thought you'd like them.'

I sat and crunched biscuits and thought of a film star who had everything and nothing; a character who might or might not be her husband, who was out to kill her; two goons who tried to get me; a blind man with a stick who could shoot accurately in the dark; and an accident over an elevator that got someone in my own building rubbed. I gave it up in the end. I had a pretty full schedule this year and I couldn't spare the time.

Stella sat and watched me over the rim of her cup with that marvellous tact of hers and said nothing. Presently she got out her scratchpad and I gave her the story. She didn't say anything for a bit. I left the part about the two strong-arm boys until the end. Her eyes were wide as I finished.

'All part of the same pattern, Mike,' she said.

'Looks like it,' I said.

Stella frowned. She tapped with her gold pencil against very white teeth.

'You think this might be tied up?' she said. 'I mean the people trying to get you and the attempts on Candy Barr.'

I put down my cup and rummaged about in the biscuit tin again. For the next minute I concentrated on a coconut fudge delight. It really lived up to its title.

'Pretty offbeat,' I said. 'A famous movie star and an obscure private eye. What would be the link?'

Stella snorted.

'We've got a good motive in Candy Barr's case,' she said. 'There might be a link you don't know about. Besides, you've dealt with crazier things. Remember that time you were mistaken for somebody else?'

'You've got a point, honey,' I said. 'There was someone watching me up at Gramercy Court. When I was checking the garage. He got out too quick for me to see who it was.'

'There you are, then,' said Stella quietly.

I shook my head.

'I can't see it for the moment,' I said. 'We got one lead though.'

I got out the piece of crumpled pasteboard from my pocket and flipped it over to her. She studied it for a moment or two in silence.

'I found it by the car last night,' I said. 'It must have fallen out the fat boy's pocket when I took his handkerchief.'

Stella flipped the card back to me.

'What do you expect to find up there?' she said.

I shrugged.

'What have I got to lose by checking? If you've got any better leads, let's have them.'

'I'm just warning you to be careful,' Stella said.

I didn't answer that. Stella had been warning me as long as I could remember. I looked at the card again. Rainbow Lake, I remembered was a place up in the mountains about forty miles north-east of L.A. I wondered what the connection could be between the pug and a setup like that. Their rates were pretty plushy. I decided to look up there today. I made my living by being nosey. And apart from raking around Roy Lawrence's bedroom, which I didn't expect to produce anything, I had nothing else to do.

The card promised fishing, canoeing, speedboating and water-skiing and a lot of other delights. The proprietor was apparently a character called Ed Rumbelow.

Stella got up while I was looking at the card and took my cup for a re-fill. She came back again and put the coffee down in front of me. She leaned over the desk and snapped the lid of the biscuit-tin shut. She whipped out again just too quick for my sharp sideways lunge.

'Your reflexes are getting slow, boy,' she said. 'Too much coffee, too many biscuits. We don't want any pear-shaped P.I.s around L.A.'

'I'm not likely to get pear-shaped the miles I walk,' I said.

Stella frowned like she was giving serious consideration to my conversation.

'I was thinking of the future,' she said.

'You still going to be around in the future?' I said.

Stella looked at me innocently.

'As long as it takes,' she said mysteriously.

I changed the subject. I always feel uneasy when Stella gets on that tack.

'What about the Blind Institute?' I said.

'I made a few discreet calls,' Stella said. 'Everything seems above board. The Superintendent is a man called Edmund

Waxlow. You think you ought to go see him?'

'It wouldn't hurt,' I said. 'Especially if he's got a blind homicidal maniac with a limp among his inmates.'

'With radar-controlled bullets in his gun,' Stella said.

I sat back at the desk and made the coffee last.

'I'll phone in tonight,' I said. 'I'll take in Waxlow before lunch and look up at Rainbow Lake this afternoon.'

Stella took the advertising card from me and put it among her material for filing.

'You'd better sign my salary cheque before you take off,' she said. 'Just in case you don't make it back.'

'You're getting sentimental,' I told her.

She was still smiling as I closed the door behind me.

2

Dr Edmund Waxlow was in when I got to the Runstedt Institute for the Blind. I gave my name to a severe-looking woman of about fifty with a grey screwed-up bun at the back of her head and gold-rimmed pince-nez that made her look like a third-rate re-run of *Arsenic and Old Lace*. The sunlight spilling in through the stained-glass windows of the hall sent beams dancing from her glasses. That was the only sunny thing about her.

'I don't know whether the doctor's busy,' she said in a worried-sounding voice. 'What did you say you wanted?'

'I didn't,' I said. 'But I think Dr Waxlow will see me all right. I'm not selling anything.'

There was a pink flush showing now behind the secretary's ears.

'I never supposed it for one minute, Mr Faraday,' she said. There was mild reproof in her tones. 'But we have to be so careful here.'

She didn't say why. Unless she was referring to the shoot-out on the staircase. That would have shaken up institutions less formal than the Runstedt set-up. The grey-haired woman screwed up her face like she was going to cry. She hovered on one foot at the bottom of the staircase.

'You might ask him,' I said. 'We can take it on from there.'

A faint tapping noise came from somewhere along one of the corridors with their heavily waxed floors. I felt the hair at the back of my neck beginning to crawl again. The secretary consulted a small gold watch with a gold strap.

She sucked her teeth unpleasantly.

'I don't suppose it will do any harm,' she said. 'Classes are changing over.'

She looked at me conspiratorially, her icy manner relaxing.

'Let's risk it, shall we?'

'I'm game if you are,' I said, entering into the spirit of the thing.

The grey-haired woman was already trotting up the staircase when I joined her. I kept at her heels. The building was full of the hum of conversation and faint rustling noises as people milled along the corridors. Now we were up on the first floor I could see the patients were mostly middle-aged men. Almost all of them wore dark glasses and all wore white linen jackets cut to a uniform pattern.

The secretary glanced over her shoulder with approval.

'That's Dr Waxlow's idea,' she said. 'It makes them stand out better for traffic.'

She wheeled smartly to the left and opened a white-painted door that had PRIVATE stencilled on it in gold leaf. She waited until I'd followed her in and then closed it behind us. She paused several doors down the corridor.

'Wait here,' she whispered.

She tapped on the door and went in, leaving me to admire the lime-green walls and the cheering selection of Hogarth prints in gold frames. I went on over. They had everything there, ranging from Gin Lane to his hospital and poorhouse studies. By the time I'd finished it almost seemed like an advantage to be blind in a place like this.

The grey-haired woman was back again at my shoulder. She looked surprised.

'Dr Waxlow will see you now,' she said.

'It wasn't so very difficult was it?' I said.

The secretary briefly de-frosted her features and gave me a smile at least five millimetres wide.

'Dr Waxlow is waiting,' she breathed.

She held the door open for me and closed it again as I went in.

CHAPTER TWELVE

1

The Edwardian stained glass that encrusted the Runstedt Institute ran riot in here. Waxlow's office was like something out of a Hollywood horror movie. Oak panelling so dark that you couldn't see the walls; there were only two lamps in the room. One overhead threw a leprous light on a moth-eaten grey carpet. The other, in a green shade, was on Waxlow's desk and seemed to make the room even darker.

The stained glass at the windows was mainly blue, green and red and it translated the harsh sunlight of L.A. into cadaverous colours so that one's face either resembled a corpse; a person dying of asphyxia; or a traffic accident. That was according to where one sat. The doctor's face was mostly green all the while I was there. I guess my face was little better.

The pictures made by the stained glass were mainly religious; the subjects were things like the Martyrdom of St Sebastian; the Flight Into Egypt; and something that looked like the Rape of the Sabine Women. Leastways, there was a lot of burning going on in the background and burly women with thighs like cart-horses being roped like it was a rodeo.

Whatever it was, it didn't add up to a general feeling of hilarity.

There were a few filing cabinets in the place; a couple of pallid busts on stands; and the remains of someone's morning coffee-break on a tray that stood on a side-table. A half-eaten sandwich lay on a green-tinted plate on one side of Waxlow's desk and looked like Exhibit A in some case at night court. I looked round for the steam-organ. That was about the only thing they'd left out. I was almost up to the desk now and a figure was composing itself in the gloom.

A wheezy sigh broke the silence as the figure in the brown leather swivel-chair spoke.

'Won't you sit down, Mr Faraday?'

I lowered myself into the heavily overstuffed wing-chair and strained my eyes to make out the face of the Superintendent. He was a big fat man who seemed to go straight down, from the top of his squat head to his feet. That might have been libellous because I couldn't see all of him. But from what went on above the waist he was strictly geometrical. His hair, clipped close to the head, might have been ash-grey except that there were stripes of blue and red across it from the window behind him.

There was a green halo on one of the religious figures that just about ringed his head; that was pretty inappropriate too but it lightened up my morning a little. As far as I could make out he had a flabby, creased face

107

that was as grey as his hair. His teeth were palpably false and clicked and wheezed audibly whenever he spoke. He wore a pair of narrow, square spectacles that reinforced the impression of cubism; these had a thick black ribbon that ended up somewhere around his waistcoat.

His nose was big and mottled with drink; he had a Kaiser Wilhelm moustache that failed in its effect and red, full lips that were constantly in motion, like his teeth were hurting him. He had on a grey suit so loose that it just sat like sacking, draped squarely from his fleshy shoulders. He looked remarkable but he was pretty ordinary I found later.

He folded fingers as fat and square as cigar-cases on the blotter in front of him and frowned heavily through the gloom in my general direction. It was only then I saw the silhouette of a parrot in a big, triple-arcaded cage on a stand near the window. It was preening its feathers and swinging gently on a trapeze perch, otherwise I wouldn't have noticed it.

'What can I do for you, Mr Faraday?' said Dr Waxlow encouragingly.

His voice was high and feminine for such a massive frame. It came as quite a surprise so I was a little slow getting off the mark. Dr Waxlow sighed again and I could hear the faint clicking of his teeth, like miniature castanets, against the rustling noises the parrot was making.

'I'm sorry, Dr Waxlow,' I said. 'It was just that these surroundings take a little getting used to.'

The fat man positively purred. He seemed to uncoil a little from the swivel chair.

'Yes, lovely place isn't it?' he said enthusiastically, his high treble reinforced by the wind whistling through his dentures. He waved one podgy hand around him like he was some Indian prince showing a peasant the wonders of the Taj Mahal.

'Beautiful work, beautiful work,' he went on. 'Look at that panelling, sir. Put in in 1910. There isn't another place like it in L.A.'

'I can well believe it,' I said politely.

The old boy forced his mind away from architectural glories with reluctance.

'But you didn't come to talk about the building, Mr Faraday?'

'No, Dr Waxlow,' I said, changing gear. 'I represent Miss Barr, the movie actress.'

Waxlow's face broke up and his eyes almost disappeared in folds of skin.

'Why didn't you say so, sir?' he said warmly. 'Miss Barr is one of our Board of Trustees, as well as her Manager, Mr Sheridan.'

He laughed suddenly, a shrill falsetto in which his dentures almost topped High C.

'But of course, sir, you know all that if you represent Miss Barr? You've come about the Open Day, naturally. How is the lady?'

'Just fine when I left her yesterday,' I said. 'About the Open Day . . .'

The fat man was rummaging about among his papers on the desk in front of him.

'A most generous benefactress where the blind are concerned,' he went on. 'Perhaps you'd give her this.'

He came up with a sheaf of typewritten sheets and passed them across to me.

'It's not till Friday, of course,' Waxlow went on, 'but I know she likes to get things tied up well in advance. She'll be speaking next to last, as usual.'

I let him go on, while I flipped through the sheets. It seemed to be a timetable for the day's events at the Institute and copies of speeches Waxlow and others would be giving. This was another side to Candy Barr I hadn't realized. But then I'd only spent a few hours with her.

'We would have put these in the post tonight,' Waxlow went on. 'But I see she's keen as usual to get to grips with things. Wonderful for a person so young. Her husband's just the same. Both generous to a fault.'

He pushed a printed booklet at me while I was still folding the sheets.

'I expect she's already got the annual report but just in case she's mislaid it, here's a spare.'

I was beginning to feel like a tourist at a museum bookstall. I thanked the doctor and put the booklet in my pocket together with the other stuff.

'There's something I'd like to ask you, doctor,' I said.

Waxlow clicked his teeth gently as he peered in my direction.

'I'm here to help, Mr Faraday,' he said.

The parrot made a low shuffling noise on its perch near the window. Waxlow had slightly shifted his position in the chair and the halo was now at a rakish angle. I had a job to keep my face straight.

'I had a buddy who got wounded in the war,' I said. 'He was lame. Later he went partly blind. Last I heard he was in an institution somewhere around L.A. I just wondered whether he might be among your patients.'

Waxlow took off his square spectacles and polished them on a large silk handkerchief he got out of his trouser pocket.

'We have four or five lame men here among our flock,' he said. 'One or two partly sighted. I'd be glad to help if I could. What was his name?'

'Kronfeld,' I said.

Waxlow shook his head. He sighed wheezily for the third or fourth time since I'd come in.

'The name doesn't ring a bell,' he said. 'And I know most of the people here by name. Would you like me to look him up in the register?'

'Don't bother,' I said. 'Perhaps I could look around for a bit? I'd know him if I saw him.'

The chair creaked as Dr Waxlow shifted his position.

'By all means, Mr Faraday,' he said. 'Miss Vavasour will show you the way. You'll excuse me for not accompanying you. I have much to occupy my time.'

He looked wistfully at the half-eaten sandwich on his desk. I heard a bell ring in the far distance as his finger stabbed a button. The door in rear of me opened and the grey-haired woman poked her head around.

'Miss Vavasour, Mr Faraday is the personal representative of Miss Barr,' Waxlow clicked. 'I'd like you to make him at home and show him anything he'd like to see.'

'By all means, doctor,' the Vavasour character said. There was a decided change in the tones of her voice. I was already on my feet.

'Many thanks, doctor,' I said.

Waxlow gave me a limp, flabby hand to shake. He didn't get up from the desk.

'Only too happy,' he dribbled.

He put the square spectacles back on his blotchy nose.

'Please give my regards to Miss Barr.'

'I'll do that,' I said.

The parrot gave a disgruntled squawk as I walked toward the door. I looked back once. Waxlow already had his hand round the half-eaten sandwich. The halo on the window behind him was way down below his ears now.

I grinned. I went on out and left him there among the busts and the stained glass.

2

The Vavasour woman was a little more amenable as we went down the corridor. Some of the frost had melted from her voice.

'Would you like to see the folk-art rooms, Mr Faraday?' she said.

We went up on the third floor where about thirty or forty blind men in white jackets were working looms and doing other highly skilled work. There was a hell of a racket from the machinery. I spent about an hour there but I didn't learn much. I saw three crippled men, one weaving carpets, the others doing something concerned with printing the Institute's Braille magazine.

The first man had a special boot on his right leg. I could only see the boot sticking out from behind a loom at first. My interest must have registered on my face because the secretary looked at me curiously. When we got round the other side of the loom I saw the character was over sixty and corpulent. He didn't fit the bill at all.

We went on down through another two rooms until we got to the place where the magazine was printed. I was so sorry for the people in the Institute that I almost forgot why I was there.

'Their life isn't really so bad, Mr Faraday,' the grey-haired woman said. Her voice was low and gentle. 'Imagine what would have been their lot a hundred years ago.'

'Sure,' I said.

There was more to Miss Vavasour than I'd imagined. Close up she was a lot more human. We were in the printing shop now. Both the men I was interested in were completely blind. One had an arthritic hip, the other a steel gadget on his leg, the disability the result of polio as a child. I didn't stay long. The place was beginning to depress me. The slamming noises from the print-shop died away as we went down the corridor outside.

'It must be interesting representing Miss Barr,' the Vavasour woman said.

There was a wistful tone in her voice and I suddenly caught the whole picture of her life.

'It has its disadvantages, Miss Vavasour,' I said. 'Your set-up here is so much more worthwhile.'

The grey-haired woman's face lit up. It changed the whole aspect of her personality. Even her voice sounded younger as she replied.

'Do you really think so, Mr Faraday?'

We were still walking down the corridor but now we stopped for a moment, though neither of us had made any outward gesture.

'Sure,' I said. 'Film stars come and go, but the work of the Institute goes on for ever.'

114

The secretary smiled again.

'That's true,' she said.

'Besides,' I told her. 'Actresses get old or have accidents. All life's a matter of luck.'

I glanced round the corridor with its shining linoleum and bleak walls. I didn't sound very convincing even to myself but I'd started now and I had to go on.

'All this isn't wasted,' I said. 'It's better than politics. Better than many other vocations.'

The secretary didn't say anything. She turned away but I could see from the set of her back that I'd said the right thing. I decided to leave it at that. I was waiting for Miss Vavasour to open another door when I heard a familiar sound.

A tapping noise was coming toward me from a corridor somewhere up ahead. Underneath it I could hear the slurred dragging of a foot along the linoleum. The pressure of the Smith-Wesson against my chest increased as I turned to face the sound. I waited expectantly, a muscle twitching in my cheek, as the noises came nearer.

CHAPTER THIRTEEN

1

The seconds crawled by as slowly as the dragging foot. The Vavasour woman's face registered only mild curiosity as she waited, one hand on the door-handle. A long shadow slid across the linoleum as the blind man paused at the intersection of the two corridors. He hesitated for perhaps thirty seconds and then the tapping of the stick started again. The shadow rippled across the floor and flickered out on the opposite wall.

The secretary still didn't say anything. I waited for another fifteen seconds. Then the stick-tapper came in sight. He was tall and, as far as I could make out under his dark cheaters, about thirty-five years old. He had a muscular frame and I soon saw he didn't really need the electronic stick because he was blind. There was a plaster cast on his right leg and it was the metal frame round his leg to protect the plaster which dragged along the floor.

He supported himself on the stick and I could see by the way he moved his head that he was partly sighted. He had on the white jacket worn by the other inmates of the Runstedt Institute but the striped pyjama trousers looked incongruous. The right leg of the pyjamas had been cut away to accommodate the cast. He looked like a pretty unlikely candidate for my murder attempt but I earned my living by being suspicious and until it was proved otherwise he was my number one suspect.

He had a hard, tanned face and his nose had been broken at one time or another. His hair was dark and grew thickly over his scalp and was fashionably trimmed with a razor. He wore a red- and green-striped tie and a cream shirt under the white jacket, which made him look something like an English cricketer. Leastways, those I'd seen played by people like C. Aubrey Smith and David Niven. He had lean, tight lips which were pursed over strong white teeth.

He paused again at the end of the corridor and then came rather hesitantly toward us, dragging his foot almost thoughtfully; supporting himself with the stick and bringing his left leg up until he was ready to move forward again.

'This is Mr Dillingham,' the Vavasour woman whispered in my ear. 'He had a bad motor accident and broke a leg.'

'I can see that,' I said. 'I hope he was a passenger and not driving.'

The secretary shook her head like I was short on grey matter.

'You don't understand, Mr Faraday,' she said. 'Mr Dillingham came here before that.

He's partly sighted. He was a professional boxer and his eyesight started failing after he was knocked out in a bout.'

I remembered where I'd seen him then. I'd caught a couple of his fights three or four years earlier. Even then he was a bit elderly for a pro. He was making a come-back. He needed the money I guess. Like most professional pugs who never seem to put anything by for their old age. The secretary kept on whispering as Dillingham continued shuffling toward us.

'The doctors don't quite know what the trouble is but they hope it's only temporary.'

'So he can see?' I said.

The grey-haired woman shrugged.

'Sometimes perfectly normally. At others a sort of curtain seems to come down. It starts with a mist and within an hour or so he's completely blind. On other occasions he's half-sighted for days and then his vision clears again. There's some pressure, evidently . . .'

She didn't have time for any more because Dillingham was up with us now. He paused hesitantly and peered in our direction.

'I'm sorry,' he said in a strong, clear voice. 'I can only see a vague blur.'

'It's all right, Mr Dillingham,' the secretary said. 'It's me, Miss Vavasour. And a visitor.'

Dillingham chuckled. He gave me a hard, horny hand to shake.

'Faraday,' I said. 'Pleased to know you. I

caught a few of your fights.'

The big man's delight was genuine.

'You see me fight Pinky McClain? Now that was one. Down in four.'

He sighed.

'Those were the great days.'

There was an ugly silence, broken by Miss Vavasour's brisk voice.

'Nearly lunch-time, Mr Dillingham. You don't want to be late.'

'I'm just on my way there,' the big man said. 'You want to come along?'

He was talking to me and the two of us fell in beside him and adapted our walk to his painfully slow progress. I was only about two feet from Dillingham and I studied his face carefully. He seemed to be exactly what he purported. Whatever it was, I couldn't find any flaw in his story or his being there. I could check with Waxlow later; make sure his medical records were genuine. Though what purpose anyone would have in masquerading as a blind man and gaining admittance to the Institute was beyond me. I gave it up for the time being.

He kept on about the fight game and the Vavasour woman didn't try to stop him. He looked pretty fit still and it came out during his conversation that his blindness had only come on during the last year. The car accident, on an outing from the Institute, had happened a month before. We got in an elevator at the end

119

of the corridor and ground slowly down to street level.

I thought it was about time I got out. I'd learned all I'd come to learn. Which was precisely nil for the moment. Though there was still a question over Dillingham. The secretary pressed me to stay to lunch but I cried off. Dillingham shook hands again. He looked at me wistfully.

'I'd sure like to be outside again,' he said.

'You will be,' I told him.

I left him standing there at the dining-room entrance and found my way back to the marble lobby and the street.

2

Rainbow Lake Lodge was about a two-hour drive up into the mountains and it was already three-thirty in the afternoon when I got there. The snow on the top of Mount Baldy was almost invisible in the industrial haze over L.A. far away as I tooled the Buick off the main stem and over a secondary tarmac road that looped around the lake.

It was a pretty nice spot up here, relatively undeveloped and unspoiled, with only a few week-end cottages and cabins dotted about. A white-boarded sign-post said: RAINBOW LAKE 5 Miles, as the Buick's wheels rumbled over a heavy timber bridge. Down below the piles icy water ran in white foam, tumbling over boulders until it was lost in a misty gorge. As I cleared the bridge the sun filtered down through the woods and vivid blues, reds and greens made a halo in the spray. I guessed that was what gave the lake its name.

I almost ran the Buick off the road when I spotted that big coloured arc floating up over the tree-tops. Then the rainbow was cut off by a curve of the road and I was out again into blinding sunshine, the tarmac road straight and narrow now along the lake shore. The tyres sang on the rough surface and the wind whipped whitecaps from the cold, green surface of the lake, bobbing flocks of red-hulled sailboats as they went about.

Farther out the white wake of a speedboat made an S-shaped scar on the surface of the water and people were diving from anchored pontoons; the far shore of the lake was a dim blue and I could see the faint dots of fishermen sitting on the rocks, their rods making sharp angled strokes against the light-coloured background.

It seemed to me to be a bit early for swimming up here but maybe the water was warmer than it looked; or perhaps they bred a hardy type of holiday-maker. The Buick was running close to the nearer shore and beaches of white sand were coming up. I passed two or three hotels built in the style of Swiss chalets but even they didn't spoil the scene. The car-parks were back in the woods, screened by trees. A wooden pier ran out into sparkling blue water now I was round the point and then the lake widened out into a sort of bay.

There was a small town here and I slowed down, the car bumping over artificial ridges in the road put there to keep traffic speed at a minimum. There were decently built houses, mostly of solid granite from the edge of the lake; and their well-shaved turf re-echoed the colour of the lake water farther out. I passed a group of blonde girls riding ponies, their yellow jodhpurs and red sweaters making vivid splashes of colour against the surface of the highway.

Then I turned and bumped gently uphill, past a screen of ornamental bushes over a minor road that was edged with boulders painted white. Another big sign said: RAINBOW LAKE LODGE. I could hear the putter of outboard motors now and once a water-skier went by, the spray coming up like smoke from his feet, the line attaching him to the launch invisible against the surface. He was making some pretty fancy scissor movements until he took a header and disappeared in a vicious whirlpool of broken water.

I sighed at all this evidence of leisure and fought the Buick up the last half-mile to where the imposing bulk of the lodge reared against the trees. I drove through an archway made of wrought iron and on into a horse-shoe shaped concourse floored with pink gravel. I parked up against a rough stone wall topped with boxes of scarlet flowering plants and walked back over toward the entrance.

The Lodge was an enormous place built in a semicircle, mostly of rough stone from the lake-shore with plenty of cedar and plate glass. It was really an hotel and had something like two hundred rooms though it was early in the season and there couldn't have been more than fifty or sixty people staying there. There was a fine view of the lake from here; it was spread out like a vast shield about two hundred feet below.

The hotel was built on a sort of dogleg so that it commanded the whole sweep of the lake where it turned in a vast U; the half-moon shape of the hotel meant that each side had an equal view. The front wing looked across to the far shore. There must have been uninterrupted stretches of water for about seven miles in each direction.

I hadn't come for the view though, so I went on up the three-tiered granite steps. I went on through the big plate-glass doors framed in burnished steel and fought my way through the crowds across a concourse tiled with ceramic views of hunting scenes. There were pine-panelled walls; lots of rough stone in the decor; and the stuffed heads of moose and other game animals hanging about here and there. It looked too much like a political convention for my taste.

The reception desk was a huge oval thing got up with rough-hewn timber like a log cabin. There were two or three clerks behind it dressed in Western-style jackets with string ties. They probably had boots with spurs but the counter was too high for me to make sure. A tall man with blue eyes set in a tanned, friendly face stopped sorting messages and came on over as I got up to the desk.

'Welcome to Rainbow Lake Lodge,' he said in a soft, southern voice.

'You certainly go in for the gracious treatment,' I said.

The reception clerk grinned.

'We sure aim to please,' he said. He looked round like he was afraid we might be overheard.

'Leastways that's what the management impresses on us. What can I do for you?'

'I'm looking for Mr Rumbelow,' I said. 'I believe he's the proprietor.'

The reception clerk eyed me up and down soberly.

'That's about it,' he said. 'Started with a couple of chalets and the game concession, so they tell me. Look at it now.'

He spread out his hand to indicate the crowds milling about the lobby. He grinned again.

'Course that was in the twenties and I hear he had a pretty hard time of it the first few years. Now he's almost too old to enjoy it.

That's life.'

'It's an interesting story,' I said. 'But I'd still like to see him.'

The clerk blinked like he was coming out of his twenties flashback.

'Surely,' he said. 'He just stepped out for a bit. You know the area?'

I shook my head.

'Just got here,' I said.

The clerk shrugged with a sorrowful expression.

'Too bad,' he said. 'Rainbow Lake's got everything. Anyways, you can't miss the East Pier.'

He pointed out over my shoulder. Through the window the lake wound its dazzling way. I could see the faint filigree work of a boardwalk about half a mile down. The pier ran at an angle straight out into the lake. The sun was so bright on the water that the silhouettes of the boats tied up along the pier's length were almost burned out.

'Mr Rumbelow's down there,' the clerk said. 'Checking over the speedboats. We get a lot of accidents each year.'

He paused for me to say something. I didn't, so he went on.

'Mr Rumbelow likes to oversee everything himself.'

'That isn't always a bad thing,' I told him.

The clerk shrugged again. He looked around the lobby with a thin smile.

'Catch me worrying about every half-bit detail if I had all this.'

'Maybe it's because he pays attention to detail that he's got all this,' I said.

The clerk grinned again suddenly.

'You may be right, sir,' he said. 'You checking in for a stay?'

'I don't know yet,' I said. 'I'll let you know after I've seen Mr Rumbelow.'

I went on down toward the entrance again and turned right along the lakeshore drive. The whole place was laid out regardless of expense. Either Mr Rumbelow was a millionaire or the resort had been planned by a syndicate. It reeked of money. I counted at least three swimpools and notices directed one's attention to a golf-course; heli-port; riding stables; squash; water-skiing; speedboats; and a sailing club. There were also four or five separate restaurants dotted about the grounds to catch the passing trade.

I went down another flight of steps and turned toward the shore; this section was forbidden to cars. It was a pleasant place, with shaven turf edging the gravel walk and a white-painted marine railing along the lakeside. Beyond the railing the terrain dropped fairly steeply, over rocks to the water itself. The water was a cool green inshore, shading to blue farther out and the wind blew cool and fresh from off it.

Winding paths radiated from the main walk

here as I got farther up toward the pier, and snaked between the trees. There were substantially built chalets on the higher ground beneath the trees. I figured these were either guest cabins or perhaps accommodation for staff. The waters of the lake slapped restlessly against the jumbled rocks of the shore and a helicopter chopped its way noisily up wind, presumably on its way back to L.A.

I lit a cigarette and walked on, thinking of nothing in particular and taking in the lake and the distant mountains and the sparkle of the sun on the water. So I didn't really pay much notice to a figure in a grey waterproof jacket who was walking along a path under the trees almost parallel with me. I glanced at him casually and then turned away. I went over to the railing and stared out across the lake, trying to disguise my height and hoping I hadn't been recognized.

Unless my eyesight was failing, the man making like a tourist out for a stroll on a sunny afternoon was the big pro with the dead eyes who'd tried to kill me with the wire loop the night before.

CHAPTER FOURTEEN

1

I waited another ten seconds and then turned slowly around. It was the big man all right. He hadn't seen me. He kept on walking slowly along the path as though he had a definite destination. I watched him until he was almost out of sight among the trees and then I followed, keeping a good distance between us. I got over the other side of the road and on to the turf so my movements would be noiseless. I could see the big man's grey waterproof now, dappled with stripes of shadow and sunlight, as he went on through the trees.

I kept plenty of undergrowth between us. I found a curved path that twisted around the tree-boles and found it easy to keep tabs. There was no-one else about in this area of woodland and the big man didn't look around once. He went on, walking quite slowly, but with a sense of purpose. He passed three or four big cabins. I looked out toward the lake. We were quite close to the pier now; I could see the boats tied up against the sun-dazzle and people strolling down the boardwalk.

When I looked back toward the woodland I was momentarily dazzled. The big man had disappeared. Then I picked him up again, off to my right. He was walking up the zigzag concrete path of a cabin bigger than the rest. It was built mainly of cedar and stone and sat up on stilts in a clearing. There was a white roadster parked outside. The thread made by the tarmac of a small secondary road spiralled through the trees until it joined up with another road somewhere beyond the pier.

The big man opened the double garage doors set between two of the concrete piles on which the house was set and disappeared. I got behind a tree, risked a cigarette and waited. Ten minutes passed. Nothing happened. There was no sound except the faint puttering of a motorboat and the far-off high screams of swimmers horsing about in the water. I looked behind me but there was no-one else about on the woodland paths. The nearest cabin was at least five hundred yards away and pretty well hidden. I could only see its roof from here.

There wasn't much future in hanging around, so I worked my way through the trees until I came in rear of the cabin. I soon saw there was no entrance there. The rough stone wall went up sheer for about twenty feet and there was a big balcony running all the way around the house. I gum-shoed over until I was facing the blank, end wall of the chalet. There were no windows so I couldn't be spotted. There was nothing but a low, white ranch-style fence.

I eased my way through that and walked

slowly and carefully down across the turf until I came to the end of the side-wall. I was now back in front of the house again. I turned the corner and tried the garage doors. Like I figured they were unlocked. I didn't think the big man would have stayed around in the garage. A lot of these chalets had steps up from the garage area into the living quarters. That and the front door would be the only entrances to the place.

I opened one half of the big door a crack and slipped through. There were two cars in I saw as the daylight crawled across the floor. The lights were out. The place seemed empty. I shut the door and carefully eased the latch back. Then I got down behind the first car and waited for my eyes to become accustomed to the light. It was a big place which ran the whole length of the house. There was enough room for three cars. A workbench ran across the back and I could see the outline of a launch under a canvas cover up at one end.

I worked my way slowly round the interior. There was a doorway halfway along the left-hand garage wall but no door fitted. I padded on over. It was lighter this side. The place seemed to be used as a store room. There were boxes and crates in one section. This half was divided off by the central heating plant from which a dim red light glowed. I guessed they were still using it for hot water. The rest of the space this side was given over to a wine cellar. A flight of wooden steps led up into the house just beyond the heating plant.

I worked my way over to the cellar side. There were racks for the bottles that divided the place up into three aisles. There was a small window in back which gave more light. I decided to look around here first before I tried the steps. I had the Smith-Wesson out now and fanned it in front of me as I edged my way down the first aisle. I got to the angle and eased around it. I was now coming back up the second aisle. The bottle racks were more than shoulder height and would give me good cover if anyone came down the steps.

I couldn't hear any sound from the house except a faint mumble which could have been made by a television set. It sounded like the voices on a chat-show. Though why anyone would want to sit indoors and watch TV on a great afternoon like this beat me. I got up to the end of the second aisle when I stopped. A familiar scratching started way down in my belly muscles. The faint light from the window spilled in and picked out a foot in a black brogue sticking out from behind the bottles.

2

The music went on from the house above and with it the low murmur of conversation. I went back to the foot of the steps. There was a faint crack of light coming from the door at the top.

When I was certain there was no-one around I came back. I put the Smith-Wesson down on top of one of the racks. I went around the end of the aisle. The foot belonged to a fat man in a dark suit. He was lying on his face and he had his two hands up around his neck.

It took me some while to turn him over but I was sure who it was before I saw the congested face. The long black hair fell over the collar and the tiny blue eyes were wide and clouded with surprise. They were almost lost in folds of skin. The fleshy lips writhed back from the strong white teeth and the once hard jaw was slack. The blackened tongue, swollen almost to bursting point lolled out of the corner of the mouth.

The hands were torn and bleeding with flakes of skin hanging down; there was blood on the white shirt and the conservative tie. The pudgy man had done his last wheel job. I moved his hands gently aside. The wire was buried so deep it was lost in the thick folds of the fleshy neck. I found the two wooden handles of the cheese-cutter in the end. They'd been twisted together and locked behind the right ear so it had been impossible for the fat man to get free. He'd obviously been jumped from behind.

I lowered him back to the cement floor again and picked up the Smith-Wesson. I'd already hung around here too long. Partners had evidently fallen out. And obviously the cheese-cutting expert had added the wheelman to his list of commissions. Why, I didn't know. I would have to find out from him. I eased off the safety and gum-shoed my way back to the foot of the cellar steps. I went up carefully, testing the wooden treads for creaks. The TV music went on. I heard a popping like a champagne cork then and the voices stopped.

I got to the door leading to the house and froze with my hand on the latch. There was a second popping noise above the music and the vibration of something heavy hitting the floor. I flung open the door then. There was no more need to conceal my presence. I swore as I blundered into a piece of heavy furniture. Footsteps went rapidly across the floor from somewhere in front. I crossed a wide hallway with pale yellow walls.

A car engine gunned up as I pounded across a big living room with a pine floor and pine ceiling. The TV set went on blaring out music in the corner. The white roadster was below me, going away fast, about halfway along the secondary road leading to the main stem near the pier. The roof blocked out my view of the driver. Nice work, Faraday. I put away the Smith-Wesson and stood frowning at the view of the lake and the distant water-skiers. There was no hurry now.

I went through the place. I locked the front door first. There was no sense in taking unnecessary risks. The living room was empty but there was a red plastic telephone on a table up near the window. I unplugged it just in case someone rang up from the hotel. There were three bedrooms in the chalet. They were all empty. I found a green telephone on a bedside table. I unplugged that too. Pretty soon I'd covered almost every room in the house. There was something screwy somewhere. I switched off the TV. That was getting on my nerves too.

I stood in the kitchen frowning at the wind whipping the distant treetops. The far hills looked high and blue and impossibly distant. Seemed like the big man had been driving the white car which had taken off. Something still didn't fit. I was standing opposite a cupboard that had white plastic doors. The kitchen floor was white too. A thin thread of scarlet was crawling under the door toward my foot.

I got out the Smith-Wesson and reached for the cupboard. The big man came out so fast I had barely time to get out the way. The door screamed back on its hinges with his weight as he buckled at the knees. He knocked three glasses off the table with his shoulder as he went down with a crash that seemed to shake the building. My nerves were still dancing with the fragments of breaking glass as I fanned the Smith-Wesson around.

The big man had been shot twice with a silencer in the chest. Whoever did it must have been standing close because there were scorch marks on the front of his jacket. The bullets had made big holes coming out his shoulders. I found chips of bone and pieces of cloth on the floor of the closet. There were two holes in the wood at the back of the cupboard. The shells would be somewhere between the cupboard and the wall. I put the gun away and stood looking down at the remains of the big man.

Any chance I'd had of getting close to the man behind the two strong-arm characters was shot to hell now. I spent another five minutes going over the chalet but there was nothing there that would have helped me. I didn't even know the two men had been staying at the lodge. It seemed like they'd been called there for a meeting. Some meeting. I could get the chalet number when I left and check from the hotel register when I picked up the Buick.

I went round the place once more, to make sure I hadn't left any trace of my presence. Then I went back down into the garage, closing the door quietly behind me. I crossed the floor of the store-room and made for the double doors to the garden. It was too late to stop. I'd got almost half-way across the floor when I saw a tall man standing just inside the garage entrance watching me.

CHAPTER FIFTEEN

1

'Looking for someone?' said the tall man drily.

He had a lean, good-humoured face. He was about seventy, I should have said and his snow-white hair showed in fringes beneath his green homburg hat with the coloured feathers. There was a thin smear of white moustache under his nostrils and his watery-looking blue eyes regarded me with wary amusement. His face was surprisingly smooth and youthful-looking for a man of his years.

He wore a dark green windcheater and an expensively tailored pair of cream hacking trousers which were tucked into impeccably polished tan half-boots. He had a small cane in one hand. He tapped this against his trousers without impatience but like he was doing calisthenics.

I noticed his hands were well-kept, the finger-nails buffed and polished. There was a gold wristlet watch on his right wrist, in a case oyster-thin and obviously very expensively engineered. It was the latter which made up my mind for me. I decided to level with him. I'd been caught on one foot physically as well as mentally and now I shifted position, making my way toward him down the garage.

'Mr Rumbelow?' I said.

The tall man inclined his head but the wary expression was still in his eyes.

'Yes,' he said in a deep, melodious voice. 'How did you know?'

'Just guessing,' I said. 'I was looking for you.'

'You choose a curious place,' the tall man said. 'You're on private property.'

'I'm well aware of that,' I said. 'My name's Faraday. I'm a private detective from L.A.'

The wary look in Rumbelow's eyes was intensified but he gave me a hard, dry hand to shake just the same.

'We don't want any trouble here, Mr Faraday,' he said quickly.

'I'm afraid we've got some,' I said.

Rumbelow gave me a long, shrewd stare.

'You're going to have to explain that,' he said.

'All in good time,' I told him. 'One of your desk clerks told me you were down at the pier.'

'So you decided to look in here,' Rumbelow said with a wry smile. 'Pretty thin stuff, sir.'

'I'm afraid you don't quite understand, Mr Rumbelow,' I said.

I got out the photostat of my licence in the plastic folder and handed it to him. The old man took it outside the garage and studied it in the sunshine, screwing up his eyes like the bright light was blinding him. Then he handed it back to me.

'You've proved your identity to my satisfaction, sir,' he said. 'What you haven't proved is what you were doing in this house.'

'You didn't see who was driving the white roadster that just went away?' I said.

The old man shook his head.

'Too far off,' he said shortly. 'I came through the woods.'

'A pity,' I said. 'It might have been a big help.'

'Just what is all this, Mr Faraday?' Rumbelow said. A note of impatience was creeping into his voice. 'I came up here to find Caldwell and I find you instead.'

'Is Caldwell a huge guy with arms like a gorilla?' I said.

Rumbelow nodded.

'That's right. He runs the boats up here with Steevens.'

'Steevens being a small, pudgy man,' I said.

Rumbelow nodded again. He was getting more bewildered by the minute.

'I've got a shock for you, Mr Rumbelow,' I said. 'We got bad trouble. How long have you known these two boys?'

'About three months,' said Rumbelow shortly. 'They were recommended by one of my customers.'

'He didn't show very good taste,' I said. 'They tried to rub me out the other night. The man in the white roadster just did a job on them.'

138

Rumbelow's face registered shocked incredulity but I figured he was a tough old bird. He had integrity too. I was in a spot and I had to level with him.

'We haven't got much time, Mr Rumbelow,' I said. 'We've got to be friends.'

I reached in my nylon holster and took out the Smith-Wesson. Rumbelow's eyes were wide. Whether in fear or astonishment I didn't wait to find out.

'I'd just like you to have a look at this,' I said. 'For the record.'

I handed the gun to Rumbelow, butt first. The old man's face broke up in a frosty smile.

'I get it,' he said.

He broke open the chamber and inspected it. Then he sniffed at the barrel.

'It hasn't been fired if that's what you're after,' he said. 'I can vouch for that.'

'Thanks,' I said.

Rumbelow handed me the Smith-Wesson and I put it back in the holster.

'Just what did you want to see me about, Mr Faraday?' he said.

We were standing in front of the garage doors and his faded blue eyes looked out beyond the lake to the far range of hills.

'Funnily enough, about Steevens and Caldwell,' I said. 'When they tried to shake me down one of them dropped a card. It was one of yours. Advertising this place. I decided to come on up. I saw Caldwell walking among the trees and trailed him to this cabin.'

'You're telling me they're both dead?' Rumbelow said.

I nodded.

'Steevens strangled with wire, over in the wine cellar there.'

I pointed toward the garage entrance.

'The big man shot dead in the kitchen. He fell out the cupboard when I opened the door.'

Rumbelow licked his lips with a blue tongue. His eyes looked sick.

'Christ,' he said softly.

'We both got a problem,' I said. 'I'm not anxious for the publicity at this stage of my enquiries. I shouldn't think it would be much good for your hotel either.'

'You can say that again,' Rumbelow said. 'What's your suggestion?'

'I'm representing a well-known movie actress,' I said. 'Who certainly can't afford to get involved. Not that she is, if you follow me.'

Rumbelow scratched his chin.

'We both got good reasons,' he said. 'What we need is my friendly neighbourhood sheriff.'

He looked at me for a long twenty seconds.

'Providing you got one,' I said.

'What's the deal, Mr Faraday?' Rumbelow said.

'Tell you inside,' I said. 'We'd better go view the bodies. That is, if you can face it.'

Rumbelow smiled a thin smile.

'I've seen death before,' he said. 'Lead on,

Mr Faraday.'

The old man sat back in his padded leather armchair and looked at me searchingly. His faded eyes stared beyond me through the heavy plate glass of his office windows to where the blue mountains were etched sharply against the sky of early evening. Down below the lake was pale green now, heavy with shadow at the edges, the white herring-bone patterns of the boat-wakes looking almost phosphorescent at this height.

'You look like a man who could use another whisky, Mr Faraday,' Rumbelow said. 'I know I can.'

He held out the bottle and re-filled the frosted German glass in my hand. The old man's office was in a penthouse suite at the top of the hotel, part of his private quarters. It was just as plushy as the rest of the place. If you liked that sort of thing. I don't go in for black glass desks myself and chromed-steel Swedish lampshades but I was impressed all right.

I was impressed with Rumbelow's toughness too. He'd taken the two bodies in his stride. We weren't out of the wood yet but we'd come to a half-spoken understanding. The old man raised his glass in a silent toast.

'What's your proposition, Mr Faraday?' he

said, leaning back and squinting at the amber liquid in his glass, which he held up against the sunset. The rays through the blinds at the windows gave his face a warm pink tint.

'Let's call it mutual aid, Mr Rumbelow,' I said. 'You don't want any bad publicity for the Lodge. I don't want any bad publicity personally.'

Rumbelow nodded. He half-closed his eyes as he tasted the Scotch.

'Sounds fair enough,' he said. 'What you want me to do?'

'I was never here,' I said. 'You went over to the cabin and saw the white car drive away.'

'I did that,' Rumbelow said more to himself than to me. 'That won't be hard to tell. The truth never is.'

'I'm not asking you to tell lies, Mr Rumbelow,' I said.

The old man grinned suddenly.

'Just to suppress a few facts, Mr Faraday. I'm rather good at that in my business. Especially with some of the week-enders we get up here.'

He opened his eyes again and resumed his interrupted study of the lake. He must have seen that view countless thousands of times, yet he never seemed to tire of it. Perhaps it was because at his age he didn't know how many more years he'd be seeing it.

'Then you went in and saw the two bodies,' I said.

'Got you,' Rumbelow said. He glanced down at his wrist watch.

'I go down there tonight presumably, after dark,' he said.

'Exactly,' I told him. 'When I'm well away from here. When it comes time to tell my story I didn't see you either.'

The old man looked at me shrewdly.

'You will be telling your story then, Mr Faraday?'

'Eventually,' I said. 'But to the L.A. Police. They know me there.'

'But won't they throw you in gaol for withholding evidence of a double murder?' Rumbelow said softly.

'They might,' I said. 'They've done it before. But that's not your problem.'

Rumbelow sipped at his whisky again.

'True,' he said.

'The point is, Mr Rumbelow,' I told him. 'I'm on a case now where I don't know where I'm at. If I blow this thing now I'm in dead trouble. If I can find out who rubbed those two guys I've got something to bargain with.'

Rumbelow folded his hands across his stomach and swivelled around in his chair. His expression was blank, like he hadn't heard what I'd been saying.

'Where does this leave me?' he said. 'Not to mention the publicity.'

'You got two alternatives,' I said. 'Your friendly neighbourhood sheriff.'

'I don't exactly get you,' Rumbelow said. 'My sheriff is friendly all right—after all, my taxes go to pay most of his salary. But nobody is that friendly. He can't hush up a double murder.'

'I didn't say that,' I said. 'But supposing the murders happened off your patch? Up in the woods somewhere, where no-one would connect it with your hotel?'

Rumbelow grinned faintly.

'I begin to get you, Mr Faraday,' he said. 'Then my friendly neighbourhood sheriff could find them off his own bat.'

'Or you could ring him,' I said. 'And say you stumbled across them when you were walking in the woods. They'd still be tied to the hotel, of course, having worked here. But it wouldn't be nearly so bad as finding them on your premises.'

'I believe you've got something,' Rumbelow breathed. His face had changed drastically and his eyes were beginning to sparkle.

'What would you suggest?'

'We could wait until after dark,' I said. 'I could shift them for you. The boot of the car. Of course, the cabin would want clearing up.'

Rumbelow shook his head.

'No need to worry about that, Mr Faraday,' he said. 'I got a couple of men who've been with me for forty years. Compared to them deaf mutes would be gabby. We'll take care of that end.'

'Great,' I said. 'All I want is a week's leeway to try to crack the case.'

'You got a deal, Mr Faraday,' Rumbelow said. 'How about another drink?'

He chuckled harshly.

'Though I must be getting soft in my old age, trusting a complete stranger like this.'

'You haven't got much choice if you want to keep the Lodge out the limelight,' I said.

Rumbelow grinned faintly.

'There's something in what you say. Fortunes of war.'

He waved the bottle. I shook my head.

'I've got to get back to the city, Mr Rumbelow,' I said. 'There's a lot to do and I want to keep a clear head.'

'Guess you're right,' the old man said.

He corked the whisky bottle reluctantly.

'We're going to be pretty busy ourselves in the next hour or two. I'll see you down.'

We went out his office, through the reception area and down a pine-panelled private staircase that led to the main concourse. Rumbelow led me across between the weaving skeins of people. I guess most of them came up for meals and drinks. They couldn't all be staying at the Lodge this time of year. We almost bumped into a striking-looking blonde girl in a peach-coloured trouser suit who was just coming in through the main doors. She shot me a frightened smile.

'Why, Mrs Debrie!' Rumbelow said, stretching out his hand. His smile seemed to reach right to the edges of his face.

'I'd like you to meet a friend of mine, Mr Faraday.'

'This is Mrs Debrie. She and her husband often stay up here for weekends in the season.'

Candy Barr's lips were trembling and her dark cheaters glowed a fiery red in the sunset as she came forward hesitantly to shake hands.

CHAPTER SIXTEEN

Ed Rumbelow's face was alight with pleasure as he stood there watching us. The girl was framing her mouth to say something banal when I cut in.

'Delighted, Mrs Debrie,' I said. 'You're fortunate to be staying in such a spot.'

'Not staying, Mr Faraday,' Candy Barr said swiftly. 'Just passing through.'

'Pity,' said Rumbelow, scratching his head and scrutinizing both of us closely. 'Nice of you to look in to see me, though. Your husband with you?'

The girl shook her head.

'I'm alone today. I was only a couple of miles off the route so I thought I'd stop off.'

'That's real nice,' said Rumbelow again.

He was looking anxiously at the light fading from the sky.

'Unfortunately, I got to be away now.'

'Don't worry about that, Mr Rumbelow,' I said. 'I'd be glad to buy this lady a drink to see her on her road.'

The girl seemed to have recovered herself now. She gave me a slight bow.

'That's very gallant of you, Mr Faraday,' she said. 'There's a nice little place at the lake-edge down there.'

'That's fine,' said Rumbelow. 'I'll be off,

147

then. Don't forget to come back real soon.'

'We'll be back, Mr Rumbelow,' the girl said.

She was silent as she led the way out through the doors. She fell in alongside me and we walked back down the lake-front toward a tea-house that was about three hundred yards distant. The sun was a smoky red ball beyond the mountains now and the air came up damp and chill off the water.

'This is quite a surprise, Mrs Debrie,' I said.

The girl shrugged. 'That's a name Roy and I use when we come up here,' she said. 'It's the only way to get privacy.'

'Sure,' I said. 'Only you have the damnedest way of cropping up whenever I call anywhere. Like the Runstedt Institute.'

I got out the papers from my pocket and handed them to her.

'Friday's ceremony details,' I said.

'Something's happened?' the girl said.

'You could say so,' I told her. 'Two plug-uglies tried to jump me on the private road when I left your house.'

The girl stopped and took her glasses off. I could see the shock in her eyes.

'One of them dropped a card which gave the address of this place,' I said. 'I came on up here. One was alive when I arrived. When I got inside their chalet both were dead. A character in a white roadster drove off too fast for me to see his face.'

The girl looked drawn.

'You all right?' I said.

She nodded.

'How did you find me?' I said.

'I rang Stella,' Candy Barr said. 'I thought I'd better come up. Roy's back. I'm frightened to be alone with him after what happened.'

'You did right,' I said.

The girl smiled faintly. We started walking again.

'You're coming round to my way of thinking?' she said.

'Let's just say I've got my doubts,' I said.

The girl ruffled up the bundle of material I'd handed her.

'What were you doing at the Runstedt Institute?' she said.

'Following up routine inquiries,' I told her. 'Why has your husband come back?'

We turned in at the steps of the big rococo tea pavilion. An orchestra was playing something from Lehar in back. It sounded like a third-rate Hollywood musical. A girl in a blue miniskirt and with a blouse like someone's idea of a Russian peasant, showed us to a table. I ordered a double-decker sandwich and coffee for us both. Candy Barr lit a cigarette and looked moodily out over the reddened waters of the lake.

'Roy said the conference broke up early. It didn't sound right to me. If those two men were waiting for you they must have had inside knowledge.'

'But your husband couldn't have known that,' I said. 'He'd left before I arrived.'

The girl shivered suddenly, like the coldness of the lake water was penetrating to the interior of the pavilion. There were only half a dozen other people scattered about at the tables.

'He'd know,' she said. 'Don't ask me how. Roy knows everything that goes on around me.'

'You think he killed the two men?' I said. 'Because they failed?'

The girl shrugged. Her film-star face was a deep amber colour with the sunset. 'Or had them killed,' she said.

'It's possible.'

'Anything's possible. That's why I had to see you. I'd like you to stick close the next few days.'

'Shouldn't be too difficult, honey,' I said.

The girl looked at me quickly. I found it difficult to read the expression in her eyes. Before she could say anything more the girl from the Student Prince brought the coffee and sandwiches. I was on my second cup before Candy Barr spoke again.

'I'd like you to stay at the house for a bit,' she said. 'Roy will have to go to his office. You could go over his room. And I'd like you to be along for the ceremony at the Institute.'

'Sure,' I said. 'Why not?'

I finished off the coffee and sat looking out

150

over the lake, without really seeing it now. It was almost dark by this time and a few lights were already pricking the gloom of the opposite shore, presumably from villas set among the woods. We were silent for a long while. I finished off the coffee.

'Would you like anything else?' I said.

Candy Barr shook her head.

'That's just fine,' she said. 'It will do me nicely till I hit the city.'

'You want me to come over tonight?' I said. 'I'll have to put some things in a bag.'

'I'd appreciate it, Mike,' the girl said.

The rabbit's foot in the gold mount on the thin gold chain round her neck swung gently against the material of her trouser-suit, as she crossed one elegant calf over the other.

'Will do,' I said. 'Though how I'm going to put up with Dodo I don't know.'

The girl grinned.

'He's awfully sweet when you get to know him,' she said.

She lifted her eyes and I turned to see the waitress standing at my elbow.

'Will there be anything further, sir?' she said. 'But we do close at seven o'clock normally.'

I looked at my watch.

'The time has a habit of going up here,' I said. 'This will take care of the extra.'

I put another bill down on the silver salver the girl held out. It had a startling effect on her

151

expression. Candy Barr got up. There was an amused expression in her eyes. I followed her out and we started walking back along the lake again.

'Thanks for the refreshment, Mike,' she said.

'It all comes out of your expenses,' I said modestly. 'That's why I can afford to give waitresses a little extra.'

'I want an itemized account,' she said mockingly.

We were up near the front of the Lodge now and its mauve neon was re-echoed from the waters of the lake.

'How did you come up?' I said. 'Car?'

Candy Barr nodded.

'No need to worry,' she said. 'I checked it out. I stopped at the nearest garage and had them go over the braking system.'

'Good girl,' I said. 'You're learning. You're sure you weren't followed.'

The girl shook her head.

'Not a chance, Mike. I doubled back several times. There was nothing behind me at all the last twenty miles.'

'That's fine,' I said. 'I should hate you to run any risk on my account. We'd better stay together going back.'

The girl looked at me curiously. We were over near the Buick by this time.

'Just as you say. There's something I'm still puzzled about, though. The Runstedt

152

Institute?'

'How I got on to it?' I said. 'No mystery, really. Someone phoned me and suggested an appointment there at eleven one evening. He took a shot at me and missed.'

I couldn't see Candy Barr's expression properly because it was almost dark now but her eyes were wide with fear or astonishment.

'That means someone close to you, honey,' I said.

The girl went over and stood with her back to me. She held on to the white railings of the car-park and didn't say anything for a long minute.

'It all comes back to Roy,' she whispered in the end.

'There's a lot of possibilities,' I said. 'There's all the people at your studios. And you must know hundreds more.'

'But who else would have the motive?' the girl said in a choked voice.

'Give me a little time,' I said. 'I've only been on the job a few days.'

Candy Barr turned round quickly. Impulsively she put both her hands in mine. They felt soft and warm between the hardness of my fingers.

'I'm not criticizing, Mike,' she said. 'I'm just lonely and afraid.'

'Don't be,' I said. 'It will work out. Besides, you're not alone. Someone's made three separate attempts to rub me recently.'

I felt Candy Barr's fingers tremble violently. Abruptly, she disengaged her hands and turned toward the lake.

'There's got to be a link, Mike,' she said in a low voice.

'Perhaps the person who tried to get you didn't want any interference,' I said. 'So he— or she—tried to kill me.'

The girl turned around again. Her features were dark and indistinct now, against the background of broken water.

'He'd have to know me pretty well, Mike,' she said.

I nodded.

'That's what I figured,' I said.

CHAPTER SEVENTEEN

Roy Lawrence smiled hesitantly and put down the glass rod he'd been using to stir the cocktails.

'Nice to meet you, Mr Faraday,' he said. 'We could use some more insurance. I always figured Candy under-insured.'

'I'll look after her all right, Mr Lawrence,' I said.

He was a little more than medium height, muscular with broad shoulders that weren't out of proportion. He had a frank, open face with strong, durable features. His hair was fair and long without being too extreme. His eyebrows were startlingly light and made a strange contrast with his green eyes. Right now he wore a thin, white silk polo-neck sweater under a light brown hacking jacket. His Italian stripe trousers were impeccably tailored. His white silk socks and the burnished tan shoes gave him a very sharply turned out look.

I sat in the big rococo room at Candy Barr's house and watched him casually, watching for false notes. I hadn't found any yet. Candy Barr and I had concocted a story before we left Rainbow Lake. I was to do a three-day assessment of the property and assets. Christ knew how. I'd meet that when it came.

I'd put a briefcase in the Buick. Inside I'd

got a lot of typing paper, some pens and pencils and some impressive-looking documents. That, and a portable typewriter was supposed to convince the household I knew my stuff. I looked for a break before I was exposed as a phoney. I hoped Lawrence wouldn't be a sharp financial man. He'd know I had a job counting my change if he was. So I sat nursing my drink and thinking up my answers. There hadn't been any questions so far. I liked Lawrence, funnily. Somehow I couldn't see him hefting stone vases at one of the most desirable pieces of femininity in California. But surface didn't mean much. I'd learned that in my years on the coast. Candy Barr was up changing her clothes at the moment so the small talk was up to the two of us. The coloured girl Rita was in the big dining bay laying the table for dinner. It was almost eleven o'clock now but the hour hadn't caused anybody any surprise.

I'd gotten hold of Stella by phone and briefed her what to say. She was to phone in from time to time. If anybody asked she had the right spiel. I was from out of town, which was why I had to stay three days. And the three days would cover the Open Day at the Runstedt Institute. Beyond that I couldn't see. I felt for the moment the pressure was off. With the killing of the two men up at the lake the character who was throwing all the violence around might give things a rest.

156

Unless he had other help up his sleeve.

If he was the same party who'd tried to get me he might try for the girl and myself in one go. I'd be ready for that. And if it was Roy Lawrence like the girl supposed I was ready for that too. I was getting a headache with throwing all these heavy thoughts around so I gave it up for the night. I'd waited until Lawrence had finished stirring the cocktails out of courtesy and now I lifted my glass in salute to his own.

'You're from San Francisco, I believe, Mr Faraday?' Lawrence said.

'I've been there three years,' I said. 'I know L.A. better. I spent quite a few years in the business.'

Lawrence came over to stand in front of me. He frowned at his cocktail glass, shook his head slowly and went back over to the buffet.

He tinkled around for a minute or two and then rejoined me. He looked pensively down the room toward Rita.

'Insurance?' he said, like there hadn't been a gap of more than a minute.

'This and that,' I said. 'I used to do other things.'

'Like what?' Lawrence said.

He had an innocent smile. The girl Rita looked down toward us curiously.

'A little of this, more of that,' I said.

Lawrence laughed. He opened his mouth to say something when Candy Barr came in. She

157

had on a simple blue dress that was cut with the vee just right. She looked as fresh and dewy as a TV ad for Seaspray Talcum Powder. I grinned to myself. That's how you get in California, Faraday. Even the clichés become parodied.

'Come and join us, darling,' Roy Lawrence said. 'I was just finding out all Mr Faraday's little secrets.'

'Oh,' the girl said coolly. 'I didn't know he had any.'

She effortlessly avoided the kiss her husband was trying to plant on her cheek and went over toward the buffet and her waiting drink. Lawrence looked at me blankly.

'I thought Paul was coming over tonight?' he said.

The girl came back with her drink. She shook her head impatiently.

'He had to go out of town,' she said.

She smiled sweetly at me.

'Cheers, Mr Faraday.'

'Are you married, Mr Faraday?' Lawrence said.

I shook my head.

'I came close to it once or twice,' I said.

'At thirty-three you can afford to wait,' Lawrence said.

I looked at him for a long moment. There was only a frank smile on his face. Candy Barr was frowning concentratedly over his shoulder.

'You seem to know a lot about Mr Faraday,

Roy,' she said.

Lawrence laughed shortly.

'I'm only repeating what you told me, honey,' he said.

I glanced at the girl. There was a strange expression at the back of her eyes.

'I forgot,' she said.

'Seems like you've been doing some checking yourself,' I said.

Candy Barr smiled faintly.

'I always like to know everything about people I'm in contact with,' she said.

Lawrence made a mock-face at me.

'Everything?' he queried.

Candy Barr started to go pink beneath her tan. It looked good on her.

'You've been talking to Stella,' I said.

The girl swirled her drink around like she was tired of the conversation. Her eyes spelled out a warning to me. The dark girl Rita was at my elbow.

'Are you folks going to stand around all evening?' she said in a hostile voice. 'The stuff will be cold.'

'If it wasn't so difficult to get decent staff I'd have fired you years ago,' Lawrence said in a loud voice.

The girl Rita sniffed. Nobody took any notice.

'We'd better sit down, Roy,' Candy Barr said. 'There is something in what she says.'

Rita sniffed again. She looked at me

critically. 'You got yourself in peculiar company, Mr Faraday,' she said.

She stamped back over toward the table. I took the folded sheet of paper she'd passed me while my back was blocking out the view for Candy Barr and Lawrence. I put it in my pocket as I followed the others over toward the table.

2

The meal passed pleasantly enough. The food was excellent and though Candy Barr and Lawrence kept up a bantering conversation it was obvious to even a casual onlooker that there was something not quite right. Perhaps a veiled hostility on the girl's part; uncomprehending bafflement on the man's. Unless I was reading the situation all wrong. I wondered what was on the paper Rita had passed to me.

She'd hinted before that things weren't all they seemed out at Gramercy Court. Perhaps she'd found out something. I took the liqueur brandy from the tray the dark girl handed me and tried to read the expression on her face. That was a waste of time. She was too well-trained to give anything away. I put the glass down in front of me and picked up my coffee cup. Candy Barr and Lawrence were talking about studio matters and I was temporarily excluded from the dialogue, though not in any pointed way.

I excused myself from the table and went up to the first floor wash-room. The dark girl didn't follow me out. That would have been too obvious if Lawrence was who I thought he was. The paper had only two scribbled lines on it. They said; Mr Faraday. I must see you tonight. I flushed the paper down the toilet and went back down the corridor. There was no-one around. I went back to Lawrence's bedroom. I knew where it was because Candy Barr had pointed it out before.

I switched on the light and went over the place. It took me only three minutes. There was just a bureau beside the bed and a chest of drawers. The chest contained clothes and the bureau nothing of any significance. I took a last look around and came out, switching off the light and closing the door quietly behind me. Candy Barr and her husband had left the table and were sitting up the other end of the big rococo room, facing the open French doors and the terrace.

'We took the liberty of moving,' Lawrence said easily. 'Your coffee and brandy is here.'

I moved over to the divan beside him. Candy Barr sat opposite and toyed with a spoon in her cup.

'If you don't mind I think I'll get an early night, Roy,' she said.

I looked at my watch. It was all of twelve-thirty a.m. Lawrence caught the movement.

'We usually go to bed around one-thirty,' he said.

'When you're home,' the girl said. 'Which isn't often.'

'Hardly my fault, honey,' Lawrence said. 'I'm in the oil business, remember?'

'As if I could forget,' the girl said. She got up and came over to shake hands.

'We'll make an early start in the morning, Mr Faraday,' she said.

'Sure,' I said. 'On the inventory.'

We waited until the girl's footsteps had died away on the staircase. One of the Filipinos and Rita were up at the far end clearing the dining table.

'Let's take our drinks out on the terrace, Mr Faraday,' Lawrence said. 'We can talk more easily there.'

We were facing the faint haze of L.A. in the night sky before we spoke again. I put my glass down on the balustrade and watched the reflection made by millions of lights on the low cloud layer.

'I'd like to talk to you, Mr Faraday,' Lawrence said. 'I'm worried about Candy.'

'In what way, Mr Lawrence?' I said.

The blond man turned to face me. I couldn't see his expression very clearly because he was standing in shadow.

'Call me Roy,' he said. 'Everyone else does.'

I didn't say anything and he went on.

'Something isn't right here. Candy won't

confide in me any more. And she's been involved in two accidents recently. Leastways, two that I know about.'

'You mean that business at the studio?' I said.

Lawrence nodded. He lit a cigarette. The red glow momentarily made a scarlet mask of his features.

'Not only that,' he said. 'But a big stone vase toppled from this very balcony and just missed killing Candy by a fraction.'

'Just why are you telling me all this, Mr Lawrence?' I said.

'It's pretty obvious, isnt it?' he said. 'That's why you're here. To guard her?'

'Meaning what?' I said.

Lawrence shrugged. 'I don't know what's going on around here,' he said. 'Won't you help me?'

'I think we're at cross purposes, Mr Lawrence,' I said.

He opened his mouth to reply when there came the rat-tatting of heels on the parquet. I turned to find the girl Rita behind us.

'Telephone for you, Mr Lawrence,' she said.

Lawrence looked at me enigmatically. 'We'll take this up some other time. Remember what I said.'

The dark girl went out with Lawrence. I lit a cigarette and stared out across to the faint reflected lights of L.A. I was still standing there when Rita came back.

CHAPTER EIGHTEEN

1

'I suppose you got a reason for that note?' I said.

The girl's eyes flickered. She stood nervously between me and the French doors, keeping an eye open for Lawrence's return.

'I know who you are, Mr Faraday,' she said. 'I read about you in the papers. You had your photograph in once.'

'So?' I said.

'A private detective out here means only one thing,' she said. 'It has to do with Miss Candy. About the attempts on her life.'

'Have you told anyone about this?' I said.

The girl shook her head.

'Like I said, Miss Candy's been good to me. I want to help. She and Mr Lawrence tried to make out that vase falling from the balcony and the smash with the car were accidents. Anybody could see that vase couldn't fall by itself.'

'I know that, Miss Barr knows it,' I said. 'Where does that get us?'

The girl moved closer toward me.

'Don't get my motives wrong, Mr Faraday,' she said. 'I'm loyal to Miss Barr. Only there's something you ought to know.'

'Like what,' I said.

The girl lowered her head toward the floor. She had a strange expression on her face. I couldn't see her very clearly because she was partly in shadow but her eyes were clouded with suspicion.

'I know Miss Candy suspects Mr Roy,' she said. 'It stands out a mile.'

'What do you think, Rita?' I said.

'If he tried to kill her maybe he had a good reason,' the girl said.

'That's pretty strong stuff,' I said. 'You'd better make yourself clearer.'

'I shouldn't be talking out of turn,' the dark girl said. 'But it might be important.'

I tapped out the ash from my cigarette on the balcony and frowned across at the faint lights of L.A.

'Go on,' I said.

'Well,' the dark girl said. 'I think there's something between her and Mr Sheridan. I overheard one or two telephone conversations.'

'Accidentally, of course,' I said.

The girl grinned jauntily.

'Servants always overhear things, Mr Faraday,' she said calmly. 'It goes with the job. Besides, we're closer than employer and employed. She confides in me. She had a tough time, earlier.'

'Just what are you implying, Rita?' I said.

'Only that you ought to have a word with Mr

Sheridan,' the girl said. 'Try to find out what happened up at Rainbow Lake.'

There was a silence so deep that I could hear the faint sound of Lawrence's phone conversation coming way across from the hall beyond the big rococo room behind us.

'She been up there with him?' I said.

The girl nodded. 'Several times. If she has been playing around, then perhaps Mr Lawrence had a good motive. You ought to find out and stop it before it's too late.'

I stood there, finishing off my cigarette, listening to the footsteps of Lawrence coming back across the parquet.

'I'll do just that, Rita,' I said.

2

The main hall of the Runstedt Institute was packed with people. A sea of dark glasses faced blankly toward the platform. Candy Barr, wearing a scarlet dress, looked like a splash of blood in the centre of the platform, flanked by the sober-suited characters on the Board of the Institute. Roy Lawrence was sitting next to Candy Barr; Sheridan was somewhere in rear. He was sporting a neat grey suit today. Dr Edmund Waxlow was having a ball. He sat up on a sort of dais with the Institute's President. I stood at the back of the hall and tried to blend in with the wallpaper.

I swept my eyes slowly back and forth over the audience. A low murmuring like the sea came up toward the galleries which ran round the hall. Most of them were filled with partly-sighted patients and some VIP guests. The Smith-Wesson in its nylon holster felt bulky against my chest muscles as I focused up on the platform again. It still wanted five minutes of three. I saw Miss Vavasour in the aisle, looking flustered.

She smiled brightly.

'Always the best occasion of the year, Mr Faraday,' she said. 'You sure you wouldn't like a seat on the platform?'

'I'm fine right here,' I said.

What I was really looking for was Dillingham. I'd spotted him earlier wearing a light suit. Even with the plaster on his foot it wasn't easy to pick him out in these milling crowds. I was hoping nothing would happen today but Candy Barr was paying me to take care of her and I had to earn my fee. Though what she expected me to do in this mob was difficult to define. I sighed. This sort of show wasn't my style at all.

I went in rear of the hall for a quiet smoke. People were still coming across the foyer, through the big double doors. I decided to check on the exits. A corridor ran along here, from the foyer, flanking the main hall. I followed it down. The speeches had started now because I could hear a polite ripple of applause. Waxlow was introducing the President. This was a big deal apparently, as the applause redoubled. I peeked over the frosted glass half of the first exit door. The old boy was in full spate.

Whatever he was saying it seemed to go down well. The audience was laughing anyway. I was sideways on now and the hundreds of pairs of dark glasses had a strange effect. I went along the end of the corridor and found a staircase which apparently led to the galleries. I went back around the hall and found an identical corridor on the other side. The President was giving the yearly report on the Institute's activities. In a few minutes it would be time for Candy Barr to come on.

I looked through the nearest glass door to see how things were going. The galleries around the side-walls of the hall were almost full now. Leastways, those nearer the front. I noticed there were other, smaller sections which seemed to be empty. I couldn't see properly because they were in shadow. I felt they might make a good vantage point. I decided to go on up. I pussy-footed along the corridor and started up the staircase. It was then I heard a familiar sound.

There was a stick tapping somewhere up ahead and beneath it, the slow slurring of a dragging foot. I stopped and listened again. The noise was coming from the top of the staircase. There was a corridor there leading to the galleries. I got out the Smith-Wesson and flipped off the safety. I checked on the shells and started up the staircase, carefully testing each tread. The stick-tapping performance went on. The cripple didn't seem to be making very fast time so I figured I'd be able to spot him all right.

I was almost up to the top of the staircase by now and part of the corridor was coming into view. There were a series of glass-panelled doors opposite. I stopped for a moment near the head of the stairs. The noise of the tapping stick had stopped too. I eased forward up the last treads. The noise began again. It seemed to be about halfway down the corridor. I got to the angle at the top of the stairs where the corridor began and inched forward.

I could now see the reflection of the man with the stick in the farthest glass-panelled door. I couldn't see his feet because the panels didn't go all the way down. The character had dark glasses and a light-coloured suit. His white stick went forward again as I watched and he dragged himself slowly onward, out of my view. I shifted over and stepped round into the corridor. There was no-one in sight.

Then I saw the door swinging gently on my left, about halfway down. From the geography of the place I figured that would give on one of the sections of the gallery that wasn't being used this afternoon. It was then I decided to get the lead out. I eased down toward the door through which the blind man had disappeared just as Candy Barr started the main speech of the day. My progress was drowned in a sudden roar of applause and I covered the remaining distance in a rush.

I looked through the clear glass panel in the top of the door. It was dim in the gallery and I couldn't make anything out for the moment. Under cover of another roar of applause I eased open the door and crouched down in the gloom. The place was a small balcony about twenty feet long and ten feet wide. There were heavy mahogany railings round the edge. There was the silhouette of a man up ahead. The balcony faced the stage and I could see Candy Barr in her scarlet dress etched sharply in the glare of the spotlights, acknowledging the applause.

She was up on the dais with Waxlow and the Institute President. She started to speak again but I wasn't taking it in. The gallery was stacked up with dismantled seating and other junk and it smelt musty after the antiseptic clinical atmosphere of the rest of the place. I eased forward a little more and stopped again. I could see more clearly now. The man in front of me was too intent on what he was doing to take notice of anything else.

He looked like Dillingham. He was about Dillingham's build and he wore a light suit. His back was to me but I could see the edges of his dark glasses protruding beyond his ears. More to the point he had a plaster cast on his leg. He was kneeling, with the lower half of his body in shadow but I couldn't make out which leg had the cast. I figured it was Dillingham all right. The silhouette became elongated and then I saw a dark shadow detach itself from the man's body.

The white stick was held against the crouching figure's shoulder. I didn't get it for a moment. Then Dillingham bent a little to his right; the ferrule of the stick was balanced on the mahogany of the balcony-top. He adjusted something with a click and I saw that the ferrule was lined up on the scarlet figure of Candy Barr. I didn't need to wait for anything else. I jumped forward, caught my foot in the projecting rung of one of the seats.

The figure whirled at the clatter. I was almost on him now. I swung at him with the barrel of the Smith-Wesson. The ferrule of the stick was in the air. There was a hiss and someone down below screamed. Plaster rained from the ceiling toward the stage. People in the opposite gallery surged back from the railing. I saw Candy Barr fall to the floor; Sheridan or Lawrence—I couldn't be sure which—was lying across her.

There was a growl from the figure in front as he squirmed aside. The face was a blank; just a rubber mask. I could see the eyes faintly beneath the enormous dark glasses as he lifted the stick. The trick gun spat again but this time

171

I'd got him by the wrist; plaster rained from the ceiling again. There was more screaming now and the audience below were milling aimlessly around as fragments of ceiling bounced among them; I saw Waxlow, his mouth a black O of fear in his face, gazing ineffectually upwards.

I chopped at the gunman's wrist, felt metal connect with bone; he screamed and twisted away. His bandaged foot came up, caught me across the shins. I swung in the air, fell awkwardly and was rolling over among the chairs. The screaming went on. I struggled up, winded. The gallery was empty now, the door swinging gently on its hinges. I went at it, burst through; footsteps hurried down the corridor.

I turned the corner. There were several guests coming up the staircase. They shouted when they saw the Smith-Wesson. I spotted Dillingham then, coming uncertainly toward me. I actually had the gun up when I checked myself. He was bewilderedly tapping his way forward. I heard a clatter of steps on the fire escape stairs. I turned, saw the plaster cast lying in a corner. I went over to the metal spiral staircase. The explosion of the Smith-Wesson sounded like thunder in the confines of the shaft. The scrabbling footsteps redoubled their speed. Halfway down the stairs I found the dark glasses. There was no-one around on the ground floor. Unless you counted about three hundred blind people milling about.

I found the trick walking stick there. It unscrewed into three sections; that way it would strap nicely down someone's trouser leg. I understood a lot of things then. I fought my way back into the hall to see if I could help anyone. Sheridan met me with a dead-white face. 'How's Miss Barr?' I said.

He shook his head.

'I think she's dead,' he said.

CHAPTER NINETEEN

Candy Barr's face looked white and strained.

'I don't understand, Mike,' she said for the third time in as many minutes.

She sat behind the desk in Waxlow's funereal office and sipped at the glass of whisky. I sat on the edge of the desk and shuffled my thoughts around like they'd been playing cards. Sheridan and Roy Lawrence were outside, helping Waxlow and the staff get some order into the milling crowds. Several people had been injured in the crush. The police would be here shortly. I had to have some answers before then.

'Let's get to it, honey,' I said. 'Our reasoning's been all wrong. Both yours and mine. Your husband was down there with you when the guy tried to kill you. He wouldn't risk his own life to save you, would he? Not if he was trying to knock you off?'

Candy Barr's face changed. She tried to get up, found she was still trembling. I pushed her back in the chair.

'I've been wrong,' she said. 'I must go to see Roy.'

'There'll be plenty of time for that later,' I said. 'We've got other things to talk about.'

I looked over to the armchair where the plaster cast, the dark glasses and the white

174

walking stick sat.

'There's someone pretty smart behind this,' I said. 'Someone who knows you intimately. The same character who tried to kill me. Someone who wanted everyone to think he was a blind, helpless man who wouldn't hurt a fly. Someone who used the Runstedt Institute as a front. Someone who wanted to frame Dillingham.'

I reached out and took another slug of the whisky.

'I almost took a shot at Dillingham myself,' I said.

I took the rubber mask out my pocket and frowned at it. Then I put it with the other stuff on the chair.

'Looks like it's your turn to say something, honey,' I said.

Candy Barr's eyes were blank and opaque.

'I don't know what you want me to say, Mike.'

'The truth, honey,' I said. 'Like why you lied about Rainbow Lake Lodge.'

The girl put the knuckles of her hand up into her mouth. She looked like a frightened child sitting there behind the desk.

'I didn't lie, Mike.'

Her voice had dropped to a low whisper.

'You went up there because you were frightened I might find out something,' I said. 'Mrs Debrie.'

I got up from the desk and took a turn

around the room.

'Sure, you were up there with Mr Debrie,' I said. 'Only Mr Debrie wasn't Roy Lawrence.'

There was a deathly silence in the oak-panelled room. Choking noises came out of Candy Barr's mouth. I stepped up close and slapped her lightly across the face. Sanity came back into her eyes.

'I don't like liars,' I said. 'I can't operate with them. I trusted you and all along you were giving me the works.'

Candy Barr got half out the chair. Her knuckles showed white where she gripped the arms.

'I swear I didn't mean any harm, Mike,' she said.

'Roy Lawrence might have been justified in trying to knock you off,' I said. 'All the while you were two-timing him with Sheridan.'

The girl sat down again. Her eyes searched my face anxiously.

'How did you find out?' she said.

'That doesn't matter,' I told her. 'What is important is that you speak the truth now. What was it? Blackmail?'

The girl shook her head hopelessly.

'Sheridan didn't really mean anything, Mike,' she said. 'I admit I was playing around. Roy was away all the time. I felt neglected.'

'And Sheridan was handy,' I said. 'I've heard it before.'

I went over to the desk. I took a couple of

cigarettes out of my package. I lit one for myself and one for her. She took the cigarette but put it down in a tray at her elbow.

'You'd been up there a few times when you got a picture through the post?' I said. 'That about it?'

The girl nodded. She sat back in the armchair and closed her eyes like she was tired to death. She looked very small and vulnerable like that.

'Someone had taken pictures of us at the Lodge,' she said. 'How, I don't know.'

'They were compromising?' I said.

Candy Barr shivered.

'Very,' she said. 'I couldn't risk it with Roy. There was too much at stake. You may find this very difficult to believe, Mike, but I love him very much.'

'I didn't say anything,' I said. 'Go on. So you paid up?'

The girl opened her eyes and looked at me blankly.

'I got Paul to handle it for me,' she said. 'We got the prints and the negatives. But there were other sets. They kept on coming.'

'I'll bet,' I said. 'And you kept on paying.'

I bent over and tapped the ash off my cigarette in the tray near her elbow. She didn't move.

'How much did they take you for?'

She told me. I felt like whistling but I didn't. It would have been an intrusion in Waxlow's funeral parlour.

'And Sheridan took his ten per cent?' I said.

The girl snapped up straight behind the desk.

'You don't think Paul had anything to do with this?'

'Wise up, Honey,' I said. 'You don't think a character like Sheridan would be in a racket like this for his health?'

The girl looked sick. While she was recovering herself I went over toward the window. The parrot regarded me with a beady eye, shifted on its perch and made windy noises to itself. I came on back toward the desk.

'Did you ever see or hear from anybody regarding the pictures other than through Sheridan?' I said.

'The first few times,' the girl said sullenly. 'Afterwards, Paul showed me the notes.'

'I'll bet,' I said. 'You've been taken, sweetie.'

Candy Barr's face was a mask of conflicting emotion as she followed me with her eyes across the room.

'You think Roy found out and did try to kill me?' she said.

'I don't know what to think,' I said. 'I wouldn't blame him, if that's what you mean.'

The girl was silent for a long minute.

'The characters up at the lake were probably in on the blackmail,' I said. 'Someone took care of them.'

'Paul?' Candy Barr said. There was fright on her face.

'Maybe,' I said. 'We'll have to find out. You'd better give me Sheridan's business and personal addresses. I'll go call on him tonight when the rumpus has died away.'

I went back over to the desk and stubbed out the last of my cigarette. I stood watching the faint wisps of smoke ascending toward Waxlow's Grand Guignol ceiling.

'You told Sheridan you were putting me on the case?' I said.

The girl turned a faint pink beneath her tan.

'I may have mentioned it,' she said.

'You may have mentioned it,' I said. 'I ought to have my brains examined. Because you can't keep things to yourself someone tried to rub me—twice. They damned near succeeded too.'

My anger must have burnt through my voice because the girl flinched. She looked like a twelve-year-old schoolgirl who'd been caught stealing cookies.

'Would it help if I said I was sorry, Mike,' she said in that low voice of hers.

'Try it,' I advised her.

'I'm sorry,' the girl said.

I stood looking at her, thinking of a lot of things. My anger started to evaporate. It didn't seem to matter somehow.

'Forget it,' I said.

The girl was on her feet now. She came over and put her arms around my neck.

179

'I'm glad I put you on the case,' she said.

She kissed me on the cheek. I pushed her gently away.

'Save it for your husband,' I said.

A shadow passed over Candy Barr's face.

'Does he have to know?' she whispered. 'About Paul and me.'

'We'll see,' I said.

I went on out and left her there in the Gothic twilight with the stained-glass windows and the parrot.

CHAPTER TWENTY

Sheridan wasn't home when I called. His business place was on the third floor of a plushy pink-granite block on one of the main stems. I got there just after eight o'clock in the evening. I hadn't announced myself. I wanted to surprise him. He could have been anywhere, of course. But I figured he'd be in his office. He'd have quite a lot of things to arrange if my hunches were correct.

My experience is that a man doesn't keep his most personal things at his home; they're in his office, tucked away among hundreds of card indexes. Harder to find that way. I thumbed the button of the elevator in the Spyros Building and whined my way up to the third. There'd been no-one around in the lobby but lights showed on several floors so there must be someone about.

I gum-shoed down a corridor with a pastel-shaded carpet and searched the frosted-glass doors. Sheridan, Hardwick Inc., occupied the whole of one section of the corridor. There was a light shining from underneath the door like it was leaking through from an inner room. I tried the door. It was unlocked. That was curious. I looked back down the corridor. Apart from the overhead lighting there were no other signs of life on this floor. I opened

Sheridan's door a crack. I got inside and closed it behind me.

The light was coming from behind a glass-screened office up ahead. I could see desks and hooded typewriters silhouetted against the glow. There was only the soft radiance from behind the screen like a desk lamp was on. There was a low murmuring from the far door like someone was talking on the telephone. I padded across the outer office toward the windows. There were thick drapes covering the wall here. I slid one back, found there was a balcony outside.

I opened the French door set in its metal surround and stepped out. The glare of L.A. was stippling the evening sky with all the colours of the rainbow. There was some metal furniture set about on the tiled terrace. I picked my way through and along to where I figured Sheridan's private office would be. There were plastic Venetian blinds over the windows but the louvres were open to let in the air.

Through the grillework I could see a man sitting at a desk. He had his back to the window but it looked like Sheridan. He had a red Swedish telephone clapped to his right ear and he was talking into it in low tones. I couldn't make out what he was saying. I stuck around long enough to make sure there was no-one else in the office. Then I went back and let myself into the reception area.

I got over to the door of Sheridan's office. Like the other it wasn't locked. I opened it up and walked on in. My footsteps were muffled in the thick carpet. Sheridan didn't take any notice. He sat back in a white leather armchair and nodded at me pleasantly, like I was an old friend. Then I realized he couldn't see me properly. The desk lamp threw its glare downward over the desk and the floor area. Everything outside that was in darkness.

I had the Smith-Wesson out now and I held it close in to my jacket. I sat down in a leather chair opposite Sheridan and studied his face. He had half swivelled round toward the window and was listening intently to the voice at the other end of the phone. He didn't look in my direction again for another thirty seconds or so.

Tonight he had on a tan suit that was impeccably cut. His brown-stripe business shirt had a stiff collar and stylishly broad lapels. He had a discreet chocolate coloured silk tie, and a silk handkerchief to match peeked shyly from his breast pocket. The gold case of a wristlet watch glittered expensively against his tanned wrist as he shifted slightly in the chair. I held the Smith-Wesson down below desk level and waited.

He nodded once or twice like the other person at the end of the telephone had said something with which he agreed. His grey eyes were half-closed, like the smoke was bothering him. A thin plume of fragrant vapour rose from the bowl of his meerschaum pipe which was balanced on a metal ashtray on the top of his desk. Sheridan shot a glance down at his watch.

'Well, if you're already in L.A. I don't suppose it will matter,' he said. 'But I can't deny it's inconvenient. I had intended going out of town for a bit.'

He glanced at the watch again.

'Shall we say half an hour.'

He nodded once more. The strong white teeth as he made a wry mouth looked like some advertisement for pipe tobacco on TV. Despite the good impression he created his eyes looked worried. He put the phone down with a click and glanced up for the first time. I saw the shock on his face. He disguised it pretty well with an immediate smile, but it registered at the corners of his mouth. He got up, put his hand out as though to shake mine, thought better of it.

'Mr Faraday,' he said. 'This is a surprise.'

'I'll bet,' I said. 'You asked me to drop in, remember?'

Sheridan sat down again behind his desk. His eyes roved absently around the office, like he was searching for something. Evidently he didn't find it. He went on again after a moment.

'Even so, it's a bit late.'

He sat back in the chair and put his left

hand up on the blotter and studied his nails. I noticed his right hand was down below the desk level.

'Was it about this afternoon's unfortunate business?'

'You could say that, Mr Sheridan,' I said. 'That and some other things.'

He lifted his eyebrows.

'Like what?' he said.

'Like why you tried to kill me, Mr Debrie,' I said.

There was an ugly silence. Sheridan had a sick look on his face which he tried to pass off.

'You're joking, of course, Mr Faraday.'

'Try me,' I said. 'I've been up to Rainbow Lake, Sheridan. Just in time to see you drive off. Steevens and Caldwell were already dead. But of course you know that. You made a pretty poor job of everything, starting off by bungling the killing in the elevator. I'd still like to know why.'

Sheridan shrugged. A sneer passed across his face. He shifted slightly in the chair. He still kept his right hand down below the edge of the desk. I watched him carefully.

'Why not?' he said. 'You took a long time to catch on.'

'I still haven't caught on properly,' I said.

I stood up and leaned over the desk. I pulled back the sleeve of Sheridan's right arm. There was a bandage around his wrist. I smiled.

'A neat disguise,' I said. 'Who would suspect a blind man? It almost got me—twice. But why try to frame Dillingham?'

Sheridan leaned back and closed his eyes.

'The ex-pug,' he said. 'It seemed logical at the time. There are periods when he has his sight. He was once in a film with Candy. She promised to help him get other parts. I guess she forgot. He was bitter about that. He'd spoken about it to the other guys in the Institute.'

'So you thought you'd nail him,' I said. 'I've met some worms in my time but you top everything.'

Sheridan smiled. He fumbled around below the desk. I brought the Smith-Wesson up and chopped at his wrist. He yelped and tears of pain ran out the corners of his eyelids. The blued-steel automatic bounced down on the carpet. I went around the desk and kicked it over toward my side. I picked it up. Sheridan was still bent over nursing his wrist. He swore from between clenched teeth.

'You seem to like the silent treatment,' I said.

I put the silenced automatic down on the desk in front of me. I held the Smith-Wesson where he could see it. He was up straight now. His grey eyes were quite expressionless.

'Another move like that and you get the noisy treatment.' I said.

I waved the Smith-Wesson barrel at him. I

was still thinking about Dillingham.

'The perfect fall guy,' I said. 'I'm going to enjoy taking you in.'

'No-one's taking me in,' Sheridan said.

'You're a great optimist,' I said. 'Like you were when I almost caught you down at Candy Barr's garage.'

I steadied the Smith-Wesson up on his gut.

'You were doing such a good job framing Roy Lawrence,' I said. 'Why did you switch to Dillingham?'

Sheridan shrugged. He sat and nursed his wrist and his eyes never left my face.

'Opportunism,' he said. 'I was trying to knock off Candy, sure. Dillingham was the obvious choice once Roy started to get suspicious. But then Candy told me she was bringing you in so I had to act fast.'

'So you shot some innocent guy in the elevator,' I said. 'I can understand the blind man disguise. It was a good front. I suppose you got the idea when you were put on the Board of the Institute?'

Sheridan nodded.

'What I can't figure is the motive for killing Candy,' I said.

Sheridan licked his lips.

'I don't know why I'm telling you all this,' he said. 'Except you won't be around to pass it on to the law.'

He looked a query at me and reached out for a silver lighter on the blotter in front of him. I flipped open the lid with the Smith-Wesson. I made sure it was a lighter before I pushed it over to him. He stuck the meerschaum in his mouth, re-lit it and puffed out clouds of fragrant blue smoke. He laughed shortly.

'Money and more money,' he said. 'That's the answer isn't it.'

'It usually is,' I said. 'So the blackmail racket wasn't enough?'

'I had plenty of expenses,' Sheridan said. 'Even with Candy's ten per cent. I'd taken a lot of fliers on the horses. Some deals on the coast fell through. And there were a lot of gambling people in Nevada I owed money to.'

'So Candy had to go?' I said.

Sheridan puffed out smoke from the pipe and closed his eyes like the memory of what he was dredging up pained him.

'One big coup,' he whispered, almost to himself. 'One throw that would get me out of the red and set me up for life.'

I had a sudden vision of Sheridan walking round the lake with the girl, shuffling papers, getting her to sign forms and contracts.

'You insured her,' I said.

Sheridan opened his eyes and looked at me steadily.

'You got it at last,' he said.

There was cool amusement in his eyes.

'I insured Candy's life for a million dollars. It wasn't too difficult. All Candy's affairs go through me. Half the time she never even looks at what she's signing.'

'So you got her to sign the forms without even knowing what she was doing,' I said.

Sheridan nodded.

'I got my partner to witness them. Candy deals with dozens of business propositions every month. I go up to San Francisco a lot. I took the policy out with a firm up there.'

'What about queries on the policy?' I said.

Sheridan shook his head.

'No trouble there,' he said. 'Everything, but everything to do with Candy's business affairs goes through me. We sift it all out, except the personal letters from friends. So there wouldn't be any danger of Candy knowing what I was doing.'

'Pretty nice,' I said. 'But weren't you killing the golden goose?'

Sheridan laughed.

'Maybe,' he said. 'But I couldn't wait. It would take me many years to get together that sort of money. If I'd thrown the blame on Dillingham there wouldn't have been any queries on the policy. And if there'd been an accident at Candy's home Roy would have been blamed. The girl already suspected him.'

'And you dressed like he did when you pushed the vase over,' I said. 'You were risking a lot by using acid on the brakes, though. That might have invalidated the policy.'

'Only if I'd been caught,' Sheridan said. 'If

189

Lawrence had murdered his wife it would have washed out his own insurance cover on Candy. But not mine.'

'You thought of everything,' I said. 'And all the things that made Candy suspicious were only Lawrence being solicitous about his wife.'

I stared at the silver lighter thoughtfully. The office behind me loomed large and distorted in it. It elongated the shadows and gave a bizarre aspect to the reflections.

'Besides . . .' Sheridan said, looking down at the blotter and his shattered wrist. 'Things were about ready to blow up at Rainbow Lake. I was being pressured on all sides.'

There was some faint change in his voice. I looked at the lighter again. One of the shadows in the reflected image of the office had changed position. I whirled and brought the Smith-Wesson up. The big man between me and the office door wasn't quite quick enough. Sheridan was halfway across the desk when I fired. I pumped two shots, shifting up and over. The first went somewhere in back and splintered one of the glass panels.

The second found a target in the big man's shoulder. He groaned and spun round, scarlet spreading on his coat front. He went down with a crash. The cannon bumped and skidded its way along the floor just as something hit my gun-arm. It went numb. The Smith-Wesson suddenly felt too heavy. My fingers wouldn't hold it. It bounced on the carpet.

Sheridan's face was alight with triumph. I caught his gun-arm with my left. The silencer was pointing at the ceiling now. I found my leg caught as I tried to go forward. The man on the floor had crawled over. He cradled his arms around my ankle and wouldn't let go. I saw his face then. It was the big guard who'd been on duty at Candy Barr's gateway. I remembered the muddy green eyes. I kicked out backwards, heard him groan.

But he held on and took me with him. I stumbled and let go Sheridan's arm. I fell over the man on the floor, landed heavily. I tried to get up but I knew it was too late. Sheridan stepped forward and lifted the gun. The crack it made seemed to split the top of my head.

CHAPTER TWENTY-ONE

1

I opened my eyes, not understanding. The big man was still groaning underneath me. I struggled up. Sheridan's eyes were glazed. Something had punched a big hole in his gut. A dark stain started spreading out from the cloth of his coat. Choking noises came from his mouth. His blond, handsome head seemed to become blurred as I watched. He moistened his lips, concentrating on the automatic in his right hand. It wavered as he pointed it at me. The second shot came as a big slap against my eardrums.

A blue circle was suddenly bitten in the side of Sheridan's face. Scarlet dappled the window curtains as he somersaulted back over the desk. The automatic bounced toward the window. There was a thin crack of glass and I could smell powder smoke. A tall figure was leaning against the French doors that led to the terrace, the curtains billowing around him. Ed Rumbelow's face looked very old and tired as he stared curiously at me.

'Good evening, Mr Faraday,' he said.

I started getting up.

'I suppose I should thank you, Mr Rumbelow,' I said.

Rumbelow looked at me enigmatically.

'You'd better take a raincheck on it, Mr Faraday,' he said easily. 'You don't know why I'm here yet.'

'I can guess,' I said. 'That was you on the phone earlier, wasn't it?'

Rumbelow nodded. 'I heard just enough to learn you know too much about Rainbow Lodge.'

I grinned.

'You were too easy with the disposal of bodies to fool an old hand, Mr Rumbelow,' I said. 'Any normal person would have had the woods crawling with police within ten seconds.'

Rumbelow pulled at the lobe of his left ear with his wrinkled left hand. He smiled sadly.

'Well, now, Mr Faraday,' he said. 'It looks like I underestimated you. So you think I had something to do with the deaths of Steevens and Caldwell?'

'Didn't you?' I said.

Rumbelow smiled again. He held the big Mauser pistol easily but the barrel was pointed favouring my direction. He wore a light grey belted raincoat and from the flecks of moisture on it it looked like it had just started to rain.

'We'll take this up in a minute,' he said. 'No hurry.'

He drew the drapes. He ignored the groaning of the big ape on the floor. He picked up my Smith-Wesson and put it down on the desk. I felt like all the strength had gone out of my legs. I flexed my arm muscles where Sheridan had chopped me, found the feeling returning. Rumbelow was down behind the desk. He came back and put Sheridan's pistol next to mine. We were collecting quite an armoury. Rumbelow blew his cheeks in and out once or twice.

'He's dead,' he said in answer to my unspoken question. 'Unfortunate for you I had to intervene. I would have preferred to have dealt with him when you weren't here.'

'So would I,' I said truthfully.

I looked over toward the big man.

'Oughtn't we to do something about him?'

'All in good time,' Rumbelow said imperturbably. 'But if you want to play Good Samaritan I've no objection. But first kick his pistol over. I'll put it with the others.'

When I'd done that Rumbelow went round to sit in Sheridan's place and put the Mauser down on the blotter in front of him. He watched while I got the big man up on to a divan. He'd passed out now. I staunched the blood with an improvised bandage made from my handkerchief and his own.

Rumbelow grunted as I came back.

'You're quite handy, I see.'

'Rover scouts,' I said. 'Invaluable training.'

Rumbelow chuckled. He looked at me with approval. We might have been sitting up in his office facing Rainbow Lake and looking forward to a quiet evening drinking down at the bar.

'I've got to hand it to you, Mr Faraday,' he said. 'You might not know what's going on, but you can play a card when it comes your way.'

Rumbelow half got up and shifted the collection of pistols as I went to sit in a leather armchair in front of Sheridan's desk.

'There ought to be some liquor around somewhere,' he said.

He rummaged in Sheridan's desk drawers and came up with a half-full bottle of bourbon and two smeared glasses. He held them up.

'You've no objection?'

'I could use one,' I said.

Rumbelow poured the two shots and slid one across to me.

'We've got a bit of a problem here, Mr Faraday,' he said. 'You see, if you hadn't turned up here tonight, I could have dealt with the whole situation and gone back up the lake and no-one the wiser.'

'As it is we got a loose end,' I said.

I squinted at him through my glass. The old man grimaced as the bourbon passed his lips. He glanced over his shoulder.

'Sheridan didn't know much about liquor,' he said. He turned back to me.

'You're the loose end,' I said. 'Your part in this. You ordered Steevens and Caldwell rubbed, didn't you?'

The old man smiled. The smile looked

sweet and sincere on his face for a while. If I hadn't begun to know him it might have taken me in.

'Not exactly,' he said. 'But Steevens and Caldwell worked for me, not Sheridan. They all worked for me, Sheridan included. Incidentally, the other two are safely in the deepest part of the lake, where no-one will ever find them.'

'I knew I could rely on you,' I said.

Rumbelow's lean, good-humoured face creased in yet another smile. His white hair shone under the lamplight and his watery blue eyes were as innocent as those of a child.

'You see, Sheridan was becoming a liability,' he said. 'He was welshing on his cuts and then there was the crazy scheme about the Barr girl's insurance. I didn't like that at all. But he wouldn't listen to me. There would have been a showdown sooner or later. It happened tonight.'

He glanced back over his shoulder as though Sheridan was listening and he feared he might be contradicted. The thin smear of white moustache gleamed under his nostrils as he turned to me.

'Sheridan made a mess of everything,' he said. 'Sooner or later there would have been big trouble. I sent Steevens and Caldwell to fix you when Sheridan failed.'

'They failed too so you decided it was time to get rid of them,' I said.

196

'Something like that,' Rumbelow said. 'How did you get on to Rainbow Lodge?'

'Steevens dropped a business card out of his pocket,' I said.

Rumbelow shook his head in silent wonderment. The tall figure of the hotel owner looked supremely at ease as he lounged in the swivel chair. I estimated the space between his right hand and the Mauser and decided not to risk it. The big man over on the divan was making snoring noises through his nose.

'So you got Caldwell to strangle Steevens and Sheridan to shoot Caldwell,' I said.

'Not quite, Mr Faraday,' Rumbelow said. 'It's pretty accurate, though, so far as it goes.'

He fiddled with the gold wrist-watch on his wrist and admired his beautifully manicured nails.

'I called Sheridan out there for a conference. That was the idea, anyway. It was really to establish an alibi. Steevens was already dead. I shot Caldwell in the kitchen when Sheridan was getting into the car. If anything went wrong Sheridan was the person driving away.'

I put my glass down.

'Very nice,' I said.

Rumbelow shifted in his seat.

'I didn't count on you turning up,' he said. 'I just had time to hide in one of the closets when you pounded up the stairs.'

'And when I saw you you were going out the garage, not coming in,' I said. 'You played it pretty cool.'

'Didn't I, though?' Rumbelow said.

He looked at the bottle before him and poured another half-inch or so into his glass.

'I still don't get the motive for all this,' I said.

Rumbelow corked the bottle with the flat of his hand.

'It's a long story, Mr Faraday,' he said. 'Money's at the back of it.'

'It always is,' I told him.

We seemed to be repeating earlier dialogue. I looked at my watch. I'd only been here an hour but it seemed like two years.

'Rainbow Lake Lodge cost me a fortune,' Rumbelow said. 'I had a hard struggle of it. And there were always fresh building schemes, always other attractions needed to bring the customers in. I got over-extended.'

He gave me a long, hard look.

'I nearly went bankrupt five years ago. I'd worked for the Lodge all my life. I couldn't let it go.'

'Why not sell it?' I said. 'It must be worth a fortune.'

Rumbelow shook his head impatiently.

'You don't sell a dream, Mr Faraday,' he said. 'You hang on to it. Whatever the cost.'

He leaned back in the chair and briefly closed his eyes like he was tired.

'Anyway, this was about the time I first met Sheridan. He was a smart operator with all the right contacts. Big money people, film stars, politicians; he knew all the angles.'

It had been a long time but the last pieces were clicking into place.

'So you worked out the blackmail racket?' I said.

'That's about it, Mr Faraday,' Rumbelow said.

'We started off in a small way by Sheridan bringing people up. We had a special suite fixed up for photography and with two-way mirrors.'

'Spare me the details,' I said. 'I read the manual.'

'We selected our clientele carefully,' Rumbelow went on. 'People with big money, who couldn't afford scandal. Of course, neither Sheridan nor the hotel were involved. We took good care of that. We had our agents send the demand notes and the preliminary prints from out-of-town addresses. We hardly ever went wrong. We made big money over the years. Until things started going sour with Sheridan.'

'What happened when things did go wrong?' I said.

Rumbelow shrugged.

'One or two people wouldn't pay. We didn't want to tip our hand by sending the prints to the papers or their relatives. We had to take care of the awkward customers.'

'The lake?' I said.

'In most cases,' Rumbelow said. 'It's pretty deep, like I said.'

'It's a high price for a dream,' I said. 'You sure you can sleep nights?'

'Don't worry about my sleep, Mr Faraday,' Rumbelow said.

He stood up and reached for the Mauser. He was a tall, menacing figure in the light of the single lamp.

'We've still got one little problem.'

I stood up too. I felt cold in my gut.

'There's another one there,' I said. I pointed over to the divan.

Rumbelow stood for a long time like he was thinking hard.

'I'll figure that later,' he said. 'He'll be safe enough for the time being. I've got a car downstairs. Walk.'

2

I walked. We got over toward the office door. Rumbelow left the lamp burning. I walked through in front of him, conscious of the big pistol in back. Rumbelow was halfway through when the door flung back on its hinges. The metal frame chopped across the tall man's wrist and jammed it up against the lintel. I heard him gasp with pain. His face went grey and perspiration beaded his forehead. Stella

200

stepped out from behind the door, her face flushed and excited.

'Thanks, honey,' I said.

I glanced back at Rumbelow, pinned by the fingers.

'It's getting rather crowded around here tonight,' I said. 'How did you manage it?'

Stella grinned.

'I phoned Candy Barr and she told me what had happened. I thought I'd come on over.'

'Good thing you did,' I said.

I eased Stella forward and took the pressure off the door. The Mauser slid to the floor. The old man shook his head. He nursed his crushed fingers.

'You needn't have worried, Mr Faraday,' he said. 'There's been too much killing already. I'm a sick man. I haven't got long, anyway. I wanted to get straight with Sheridan. I was going to take you downtown for a statement. And I certainly wouldn't have started any trouble in front of a lady.'

He gave Stella a half bow. She looked at him incredulously. I stooped to pick up the Mauser. I stood there remembering a lot of things. Rumbelow waited with a sort of strange courtesy, while I puzzled it out.

'What about Candy Barr?' Stella said. 'I heard enough at the door to piece things together.'

'I think she's suffered enough,' I said. 'I shan't say anything if Rumbelow doesn't.'

201

The tall man with the white hair looked at me with his watery blue eyes.

'It's all right with me,' he said. 'I shan't involve her.'

I turned back to Stella, taking in her features like it was the first time I was seeing them in my life.

'Guess we'll leave Mr Lawrence his illusions,' I said.

'Good boy,' Stella said.

She leaned over and kissed the side of my face. I felt it all the way down to my socks. Rumbelow looked on expressionlessly. I sighed. It had been a heavy case. I looked at Rumbelow again. If I lived to be a hundred I'd never figure people out.

I pushed the old man forward.

'We'd better go downtown and get some law in,' I said.